Praise for *Five Hundred Poor*

"*Five Hundred Poor* is the type of book we need more of. Full of unflinchingly honest stories that are, at times, shockingly brutal and surprisingly tender, this is a living, breathing portrait of the world we live in."

—Jared Yates Sexton, author of *The People Are Going To Rise Like The Waters Upon Your Shore*

"Noah Milligan possesses a concise mastery of language and a sharp lens through which he sees the world."

— Jennifer Haupt, author of *In the Shadow of 10,000 Hills*

"Noah Milligan writes about Oklahoma in such an uncanny, dark, compelling way. He is a very gifted writer, and I look forward to reading more of his work."

— Brandon Hobson, author of *Where the Dead Sit Talking*


Praise for *An Elegant Theory*

* 2016 Foreword INDIES Finalist - Fiction

* Shortlisted for 2015 Horatio Nelson Fiction Prize

"... a literary Rorschach test, a mind bending ride, in which "real" conclusions are elusive, and discovery waits just beyond the next page."

— Foreword Reviews

"A vibrant puzzle of a novel, an unstoppable force—full of twists, turns, and surprises while remaining fully grounded in real life to today."

— Jessica Anya Blau, Author of *The Trouble with Lexie*

"...intrigues the mind, thrills the senses, and keeps the reader engaged straight through to the surprising ending. An auspicious debut."

—Rilla Askew, Author of *Kind of Kin*

"A remarkably suspenseful literary novel — deeply felt, and truly fascinating."

—Peter Mountford, Author of *The Dismal Science*

# Five Hundred Poor

stories by noah milligan

central
avenue
publishing

2018

Published by Central Avenue Publishing, an imprint of Central Avenue Marketing Ltd.
www.centralavenuepublishing.com

**FIVE HUNDRED POOR**

978-1-77168-139-1 (pbk)
978-1-77168-140-7 (epub)
978-1-77168-141-4 (mobi)

Published in Canada

Printed in United States of America

1. FICTION / Short Stories - Single Author    2. FICTION / Literary

10 9 8 7 6 5 4 3 2 1

*For Oscar*

"WHEREVER THERE IS GREAT PROPERTY THERE IS GREAT INEQUALITY. FOR ONE VERY RICH MAN THERE must be at least five hundred poor, and the affluence of the few supposes the indigence of the many. The affluence of the rich excites the indignation of the poor, who are often both driven by want, and prompted by envy, to invade his possessions."

— Adam Smith

# A Good Start

THE BOY DIDN'T LOOK MUCH LIKE HIM. THAT WAS THE FIRST THING. HE WAS JUST SO DAMN SKINNY, LIKE dangerously skinny, like he should maybe be in the hospital skinny, and Ralph had never once in his entire life been called skinny. A fat-ass, yes, on multiple occasions, but never skinny.

Second thing, Ralph had used a condom. He was sure of it, actually, because he always did. Every. Single. Time. Didn't matter if the girl said she was on birth control or not—he wrapped it up.

Third thing was he just didn't *feel* like he was somebody's dad. He imagined, and later on he would realize he was right, that once you were someone's dad, you automatically were beholden by responsibility. You could feel it. It pulsated. You were responsible for a living, breathing human being. His welfare and safety and security. You felt obligated. You felt an immediate sense of love and duty, but when he looked at the boy he didn't feel any of that. Instead, he couldn't help but notice the glaring absence of it all.

The boy's name was Huck, like Huckleberry Finn, his mother said, "and he's yours."

"You sure?" Ralph asked.

"Goddamnit yes, Ralph. I wouldn't be here if he ain't."

The boy's mother was a bucktoothed equestrian rider Ralph had met a decade before when she'd been in town for the rodeo. Ralph hadn't attended the rodeo itself, but the night of, he showed up to Cattlemen's, this honky-tonk dive bar next to the state fairgrounds. He'd found her there, six Pabsts in and swooning to Johnny Cash. It hadn't taken much to convince her to go back to her motel room—it had been her idea, in fact, if he remembered correctly—and after that he hadn't heard from her. And time had not been good to her. She'd lost several teeth, and she looked jaundiced. Meth, he guessed. Damn shame, too. She'd at one time had an ass to die for.

"Well, there, Adeleine, sounds like we might differ in opinion in that regard."

"Look," she said. "I was only with one guy then, and it was you. By the power of deduction I—"

"The power of deduction?"

"Yes, goddamnit. Yes!"

"And you wouldn't be offended if I said I want a paternity test?"

She scoffed, pulled out a leather cigarette case, and lit a long, skinny 100 with a flick of her wrist. "And who's going to pay for that? You?"

She glared at his trailer like an uppity, suburban bitch.

"I suppose you're the one accusing," Ralph said. "Should be your dime then."

"Listen," she said. "There's no need. I just need you to watch him for a few days. That's all. Got some business at the Winstar, and I'll be back on Wednesday. Understand?"

The boy wasn't much to look at. He didn't seem angry his mother was pawning him off on a stranger, some guy she claimed to be his father, and he didn't seem to care Ralph denied the allegations, instead staring up at Ralph like he was figuring whether or not he could take him in a fight. This seemed to Ralph to be the boy's only emotion: defensiveness. For the boy to be so guarded like that, Ralph couldn't help but feel sorry for him. He was just a sad sack of potatoes, a burlap bag covering lumpy, bland vegetables.

"Fine," Ralph said. "Wednesday then."

Adeleine nodded, sort of—she really just jerked her head down once. Then she grabbed the boy. She hugged him tight and clawed her nails into his back. She held on to him like that for a while, the boy's arms pinned to his side. Most would be uncomfortable in such a position, claustrophobic because they couldn't move, but the boy didn't seemed to be troubled by it at all. Rather, it was like he expected it—to not have any recourse for escape.


WEDNESDAY CAME. THEN THURSDAY. FRIDAY, Saturday, Sunday. But Adeleine didn't. She didn't answer her phone either, the calls going straight to voicemail. They both left message after message, Huck's tone growing from agitated to concerned, Ralph's vice versa. At first, he was worried something might've happened to her. Years ago, she'd known her way around a bottle of Kentucky Deluxe; it wouldn't have surprised him one bit if she'd had three or four or six fingers before climbing behind the wheel. But after a few days, he figured that couldn't have been the case—somebody would've tracked the boy down by now if she were dead. No, she'd run. Sure as shit, she'd hit the highway and hightailed it. For what reason, Ralph wasn't sure. Could be she couldn't take being a mother no more, the worry and the burden, the responsibility and obligation of it all. Or it could be a man for all he knew. Love, she might think it was, and her beau didn't take too kindly to children in the picture. Either way, Ralph was pissed.

Turned out, the boy wasn't that bad of an apple. Most nights, Ralph and he played cards: Go Fish and War and Spades. Games he hadn't played since he'd been a kid himself, stealing sips from his uncle's Schlitz when he was too busy staring at the weather girl on the nightly news. Ralph had always thought cards came down to one thing: luck. Either you had the cards or you didn't. Like life in that regard, Ralph thought. Some people just didn't catch the breaks.

On the eighth night he and Huck played dominoes. Huck'd never played the game before, and he fumbled around with the bones not quite knowing what to do.

"The point is to make the ends multiples of five. Five, ten, fifteen, twenty, so on and so forth. Get it?" Ralph asked.

The boy blinked at him like popping a balloon, throwing out dominoes without regard for strategy. Ralph tried to coach the boy, asking him if he had the deuce-three when it would've scored five points or the double sixes that would've scored twenty, but the kid just looked at his hand like he was trying to read Mandarin.

Did no good, so Ralph just let him play his way for a couple of hours, both of them sipping on lemonade and eating potato skins like the famine was coming, until finally Ralph just asked it:

"You got any other family out there?"

"Sorry?" the boy asked.

"Family? Aunts? Uncles? A Meemaw somewhere that still has two marbles clicking around?" Ralph pointed to his skull, but he could tell the boy didn't get what he'd meant.

The boy shrugged. "Probably. Don't most people?"

"Well," Ralph said. "You'd be surprised."

Next morning they headed south for the Winstar Casino, looking for the boy's mom. It was still dark out when they left, the time of morning Ralph's mother had always warned him about. "Just drunks and cops out that early," she used to say, "and I recommend staying away from both." In his forty-three years, he'd learned his mother was right about one thing: the middle of the night was full of drunks and cops. What she got wrong was that they were often the same people, and turned out to be some of his best friends. Maybe that was why they didn't get along—turned out her son was one of the very people she mistrusted.

The boy stared out the window like this wasn't anything new, like he'd grown accustomed to the middle of the night himself, his eyes not expectant but rather complacent, steady. Ralph found common ground with the boy. He remembered his own youth. Used to, his mother had a liking for drink and waffles, so she spent most of her time at the I-35 Waffle House next to the truck stop. Problem was Ralph's dad had skipped town a couple years before, so Ralph was forced to take umbrage in a booth, doing his social studies homework and developing a taste for decaf.

Every hour or so, his mother left him alone in there. At the time, Ralph just thought his mother popular. It wasn't until many years later he figured out she'd been turning tricks in the backs of big rigs. He remembered one night especially—he was working on what the waitresses called a heart attack bomb, which was just a gigantic pile of food: fried eggs, waffles, French toast, biscuits and gravy, hash browns, grits, all topped in maple syrup, and it was the most delicious thing Ralph had ever eaten. It was so tall he actually had to reach up in order to make a dent, and boy did he. He ate and ate and ate. He ate until he was full, and then he ate some more. He ate until he could feel his sweatpants tighten. He ate until his stomach bulged. He ate until his organs contorted. He ate until he could feel the food creeping back up his throat. Eventually, he had to stop, and he became lethargic; he became sleepy.

When he awoke, it was light out. New waitresses were working, the graveyard shift having already gone home. Someone had draped a floor mat over him as a blanket, and it stunk of muddy boots and rainwater. When he sat up, nobody paid him no mind, busying themselves with the menu or writing down an order. It wasn't until he tugged on a waitress's apron that someone looked at him.

"Have you seen my mother?" he asked the woman.

"Oh, honey," she said, her words garbled from missing her two front teeth. "Oh, sweetie. I haven't. I'm sorry."

Ralph found his mother at home, five miles and a couple of hours away by foot, passed out on the couch. She was still dressed, minus a shoe that seemed to have gone missing.

After an hour, Ralph and the boy stopped at a Love's Country Store. Part truck stop, part convenience store, there was a little bit of everything. Souvenirs lined dusty shelves: dreamcatchers, ceramic buffalo skulls, I Love OK magnets, Woody Guthrie coffee mugs, and beer coozies depicting large-breasted women. The place smelled of oil, the adjacent Subway sandwich shop, and the body odor of weary travellers. It was a place Ralph knew well, and as good a place as any to piss and grab a bag of chips for the road.

RALPH LET THE BOY WANDER, giving him some time alone. Ralph had the idea this might be the first time, but it wouldn't be the last his mother might abandon him, so he thought it best for the boy to work through it himself. Comforting him wouldn't do any good. He'd just ignore Ralph, defenses poised in prepubescent rage, and Ralph couldn't blame him for that. He knew the feeling all too well himself.

Ralph picked out some Pringles and a Diet Dr. Pepper and was heading to the register when he heard it, a scream that sounded something like a kung-fu master on a made-for-TV movie, a high-pitched "Hiiiiyyyaaaa." It took Ralph aback so much he just stared up at the ceiling, like something so bizarre could only come from someplace equally as bizarre, like a ninja climbing through the air-conditioning ducts.

"Thief!" the man yelled. He was to Ralph's left, an aisle over. "Shoplifter! Delinquent!"

Delinquent? Who talked like that?

Ralph tried to mind his own business, but the man kept yelling in that high-pitched, whiny voice until there came a voice Ralph recognized.

"Don't touch me!" Huck yelled. "Get your goddamn hands off me!"

Fuck, Ralph thought. Fuck. Fuck. Fuck.

Ralph turned the corner and found a small Indian man grabbing Huck's forearm, a couple Snickers lying at the boy's feet.

"What seems to be the problem here?" Ralph asked a little more hesitantly than he'd intended.

"This boy yours?" the Indian man asked, pointing at Huck.

"That's a more complicated question than you know."

"He is or he isn't."

"Well, then, in a manner of speaking, the boy is under my charge."

Huck tried to jerk his arm free, but he wasn't strong enough. Ralph cut him a look that said to cut it out, and Huck shot him one right back that said to fuck off.

"The boy was stealing."

"That's one hell of an allegation. You got any proof?"

"There!" the man yelled, pointing at the Snickers.

"What? That?" Ralph asked. "Some candy bars? What does that prove?"

"He had them in his pockets! I saw him!"

Ralph looked to Huck. His expression hadn't changed, and Ralph could read it as if it were in plain English: fuck you and everyone else in this world. Fuck it all. Fuck every single last bit of it until the end of the Earth. Ralph might've thought it funny under different circumstances, if it was some other poor schmuck standing in his shoes rather than himself.

"Assuming he did, and I'm not saying I believe you at all—it is, after all, your word against his—but assuming that's so, couldn't it be that he just needed his hands free to get himself a drink? Could he not have had every intention of paying once he got everything he wanted?"

"I'm calling the cops," the man said and jerked Huck's arm forward. He tried to push past Ralph, but Ralph scooted in his way.

"Whoa, whoa, whoa," Ralph said, his mind running over the laundry list of warrants he might have out for his arrest: unpaid parking tickets, a public urination charge, that one time he'd skipped out on his tab at Cattlemen's. "No reason to get hasty now. I can afford a couple Snickers. How much are they?"

The clerk eyed him sideways, squinting like he was aiming a rifle shot.

"For you," he said, "fifty bucks."

"Ha!"

The man didn't blink.

"You're serious?"

Still nothing.

Ralph did some quick accounting. He only had sixty bucks, and he needed that for the ride back home.

"I can do twenty-five."

"Forty."

"For fuck's sake."

"Forty-five."

"You can't do that. You can't go up again."

"Back to fifty."

"All right, listen. I'll do the forty. Forty's still good, right?"

The man stuck his tongue against his bottom lip. "Fine," he said. "Forty. But you only get one."

"Jesus Fucking Christ. Fine."

Ralph pulled out two twenties from his pocket, threw them at the man, who didn't seem to appreciate the gesture, and then dragged Huck from the convenience store. By this time, several bystanders had accumulated, snapping pictures with their iPhones and grinning shit-eating grins like they knew Ralph. He wanted to punch every single last one of them in their snot-nosed faces but, of course, he didn't. He only stopped one time on the way out, and that was when Huck pulled free from his grip and told him to wait just one goddamn second; he'd forgotten his candy bar.

In the truck, Ralph gave the boy a tongue-lashing, demanding Huck pay back the money he owed him, to which Huck replied that he was nine years old, "and how the fuck do you expect me to have any money?" Good point, Ralph thought.

"But why'd you do it?" Ralph asked.

The boy shrugged. "Got to eat, don't you?"


THE WINSTAR CASINO WAS A monstrosity, a hodgepodge of buildings that looked like a souvenir shop had vomited out its gigantic wares. There was a replica of the Eiffel Tower and Buckingham Palace and the pyramids and pretty much every other tourist trap known to mankind, and the parking sucked balls. Ralph cruised the rows for what seemed like an hour, intermittently waiting for some gamblers to make their exit, but they just sat in their cars, maybe enjoying a toke or doing something a little more illicit—he wasn't sure.

Once they finally found a spot, Ralph parked.

"Wait in the car," he told Huck. "I'll find your mom and bring her back."

"But—"

"Don't be a pain in my ass. Just stay. A casino isn't a place for no kid."

The kid looked disappointed. It was the first time Ralph had seen him show any emotion besides disgust and anger, and in an instant Ralph felt sorry for the boy. But it didn't change the fact he couldn't take him inside.

"Lock the door when I leave." He handed Huck the keys. "Unlock it for nobody but me. You hear?"

The boy nodded.

"Good."

The casino was dark, windowless, the air thick with tobacco smoke. Ralph's throat swelled and his eyes itched as he snaked his way through the throngs of gamblers. It was a sordid group: rednecks donning ten-gallon hats, young frat girls wasting their parents' money, overweight men with tucked-in T-shirts, and the elderly, sneaking a smoke between gasps from their oxygen masks.

He'd be hard-pressed to find Adeleine here. But hell, he was out of options.

He had no idea where Adeleine would be. He'd only known the woman for a few short nights several years prior. Back then, she'd been wild. A rodeo junkie with a cheerleader's flair, she drank and cussed like a soccer hooligan. Fun was what Ralph remembered, dumping an ice bucket full of crickets into the pool; siphoning gas out of the asshole desk clerk's car, spelling "Fuck You" on the parking lot and lighting it on fire; banging left, right, and sideways in the bathroom, the bedroom, even the unlocked facilities management closet next to the mops and bleach bottles. If she was anything like her former self, then Ralph figured she'd be someplace with the most action, getting into any kind of trouble she could.

He trekked from one shit-stained smoky enclave to another, all of it wrapped in this god-awful maroon and orange and teal green gaudiness: the carpet, the chandeliers, the flashing neon signs. Ralph had never been much for casinos. It wasn't that he was risk averse, he just felt he was being conned, from the faux gold sconces down to the free drinks and the ever-so-patient dealers, taking his money with the sympathetic upturned lip of a friend.

The Texas Hold'em room was large, full of cowboy hats and handsy businessmen, clamping down on waitresses' butt cheeks, the place vibrating with cards shuffling and chips stacking. If he couldn't find Adeleine here, he didn't know what he was going to do. He didn't have the resources to feed another mouth, buy new shoes, keep Huck bathed and out of jail. No, no matter how much he'd started to like the boy, he'd probably have to turn him over to the DHS, sentence him to ten hard years in the foster system, getting shit-kicked from one dump to the next, hoping the next one might stick, but knowing fully goddamn well it wouldn't. Ralph had known men who'd had a childhood like that, and he wouldn't condemn Osama Bin Fuckin' Laden to that type of abuse, even if his mother was Adeleine Murphy.

But he couldn't find her. Not amongst the poker tables, not shadowing some big-stacked spender, teasing her chewed-up fingernails along his collar. He didn't find her at the blackjack tables either, or slinking around the roulette wheel. She wasn't in the sports room. She wasn't at the bar. She wasn't even camped out in front of the slots, sucking on a burnt-out cigarette. Finding her was a lost cause, like trying to collect a debt from a deadbeat uncle—you knew there was no chance in hell he'd ever repay you, but you couldn't help but ask.

It was going to be a long drive back to the house, so he stopped by the shitter before hitting the road. It was rank in there, smelling of pretty much every single body secretion Ralph could think of, roasting in a pot full of cigarette smoke. There wasn't anyone at the urinals, but he could hear a guy grunting in one of the stalls. The sound he made was something canine, deep and guttural and rhythmic. Ralph couldn't tell if the guy was trying to push out a large one or perhaps preparing to bark. He wouldn't have been surprised either way, really.

Ralph figured he'd take the boy back, then contact DHS in the morning. He didn't want to do it, but he didn't really have any choice in the matter. His disability check wasn't going to cover the two of them, and what would happen if Adeleine showed back up, maybe with a couple cops, accusing him of kidnapping her kid? What would he do then? It'd be her word against his, and Ralph didn't like his chances. A mother's word was gold in the eyes of the court, at least in Ralph's experience. Best to just hand the boy over to the authorities. Granted, he'd never been one to do things by the book, but it seemed like the only course of action. Rip off the Band-Aid, he thought, and be done with the whole mess.

He zipped and was about to wash his hands when he noticed something funny: two high heels sticking out from underneath the stall door where he'd heard the man grunting. Turned out he wasn't trying to unload that night's buffet dinner but was getting a slob knob right there in the bathroom. That's when the man groaned something incoherent, a string of vowels and consonants that couldn't quite form the hard edges of language. He sputtered three times, then there was a zip, some shuffling, and the click of the lock. Ralph turned toward the sink and stared at his hands lest he make eye contact. The last thing he wanted was to be accused of being a voyeur. Never knew which way it might go—he could be punched in the gut or he could be asked to watch, neither one of which Ralph was willing to do.

"Jesus Fucking Christ, Ralph Banister." No. No. No. No. "Thought you were supposed to be watching our kid?"

"You got a kid?" the man asked.

Ralph hoped, he hoped beyond hope, he'd heard them wrong.

"Sure do. With this handsome son of a bitch right here."

Ralph turned around to find Adeleine with a stick of a man. Adeleine's voice was slurred, face bright red, mascara running down her cheeks, hair disheveled, and she stank of gin and spunk.

"Oh man, oh shit. Is this your old lady, dude?" the guy asked.

The man was smaller than Ralph had expected, given the decibel level of his orgasm, just a dry-skinned guy with dangly arms and a round paunch poking over his oversized belt buckle.

"Ha!" Adeleine laughed. "This guy? I wouldn't be caught dead with this guy, let alone be his old lady."

"My toilet's just not nice enough for you, is it, Adeleine?"

"The fuck's that supposed to mean?"

"Never mind."

She chewed on that for a while, literally, eying him as she did so. Ralph didn't want to think of what she might be chewing on.

"Where's our kid, anyway?"

"In the car." Ralph motioned with his thumb like he was hitching a ride.

"In the car? Here? Alone? What the fuck is wrong with you?"

Ralph had half a mind to defend himself—she was, after all, the deadbeat who'd left her son with a stranger, but he decided not to get into that here. It wouldn't do any good. Plus, maybe she did have a point. This wasn't the place for a child, especially one like Huck, a little bit of delinquency running through his blood. There was no telling what sort of trouble the boy was capable of getting into, and, Ralph thought with a sinking feeling, he did have Ralph's keys. He already knew Huck was capable of theft—odds of his truck still being in the parking lot may be slim to none.

Adeleine followed Ralph to the exit, the stick man, oddly, still in tow. When they made it outside, it was dark out. Sporadic lampposts dotted the parking lot, but mostly it was pitch black, the small halos of light too thin to get a grip on his surroundings. They meandered a bit, Ralph zigzagging through Ford F-150s and Z-71s, Adeleine griping at him all the while, running her mouth about how stupid it was to lose his truck, that only a moron could ever do something like that, some brain-dead fucktard not worth the two-cent boots he was wearing, yelling that if he lost her kid, she swore to God he'd pay, she'd call the FBI and have him arrested right there in front of everybody, and on and on and on, and Ralph just kept mumbling to himself that he hoped the kid was okay, please, dear sweet Jesus, just let the boy be okay. He couldn't help but imagine all the terrible things that could've befallen him: some drug-addled con artist could've broken out the window, sold him to some sick pimp trafficking youngsters across the border, or he could've taken off, hightailed it out of there with one thought on his mind, freedom, but not getting a mile down the road before getting knifed by an eighteen-wheeler doing ninety-five on the highway, trapped underneath a crumpled mess of steel and burning alive under the flames. If anything bad had happened to the boy, Ralph didn't think he'd be able to live with it. He'd lose himself on the south end of a bottle and the action end of a twelve gauge.

Luckily, though, none of that came to fruition. Eventually they came across the truck, parked where he'd left it. Huck was asleep in the front seat, his head propped up on a phone book and his hands tucked between his knees. Lying there, he looked two or three years younger than he actually was, just some innocent babe trying to cope. Ralph had the urge to scoop him up, hold him, comfort him, tell him everything would be okay. Didn't even matter if he believed it; he just wanted to feel responsible for someone else. He wanted to be obligated. He wanted to be needed. It was a strange feeling, one he didn't exactly welcome, but it was there nevertheless, like the pull on a smoker's lung tissue, yearning for just one more drag.

Adeleine beat on the window, and the boy stirred awake. He seemed confused at first, swiveling his head, trying to discern the source of the noise. When he found his mother, he sat there a moment. He looked at the stick man, then to Ralph, and then back to his mother. Adeleine tried to open the door, but it was locked. Her hand slipped off the handle, and she stumbled backward, her ankle rolling before she could regain her balance.

"Open the door!" she yelled, but Huck didn't move. "Open it! Open the goddamn door, Huck." He didn't budge. Just blinked at her. "Fine," she said. "You don't want to come? Fine then. See if I care."

Adeleine limped away, muttering under her breath. The stick man looked confused. He stared at Adeleine, then back at Huck, his mouth puckered, like he wanted to say something on the boy's behalf, but couldn't, no matter how hard he tried, form the right words. He then walked away in the opposite direction.

Ralph tried the driver side door. It was unlocked.

"What are you doing?" he asked Huck.

"I don't want to go with her."

Ralph filled his lungs. The air was cold, but clean. "Sometimes, son, we don't have a choice in what we do."

"But I want to go with you."

"You can't go with me."

"Why not?"

"Because I'm not your father."

"But Mom says you are."

"It's not that simple."

"But you could be. Couldn't you? Isn't it possible?"

"It's not, Huck. I'm sorry."

"Not even a little bit?"

"Your place is with your mother."

Ralph pointed, but Adeleine had already disappeared into the darkness.

Huck screamed. He screamed, and he kicked, and he flailed his arms about. He punched the dashboard and honked the horn and howled like a coyote. Ralph wanted to be mad at the boy, thinking it might be easier, but he wasn't. He knew what it felt like, complete and utter helplessness. It permeated him. Always had. It started out in his bones and flowed through his tissue all the way to his fingernails. He could feel it throbbing, reproducing, growing stronger, and he didn't want that for Huck. He didn't. And if Ralph was to take him, it would latch onto him, spread to him like some contagious disease. So he did the only thing he could think of: he grabbed the boy.

"You may never understand this," Ralph said. "I may never understand it. I might not ever want to understand it, but this is how the world is."

Ralph pulled the boy from his truck. Huck stood there, his face the color of ripe raspberries.

"You see up there?" Ralph pointed, and the boy followed his finger. "There's a gas station in about a hundred yards. You remember us passing it on the way in?"

"Yes."

"Good. You get there and you tell them to call the police, okay? Say you need help. You tell them your name; you tell them you're alone. They'll know what to do. I promise."

Ralph pulled his last remaining twenty-dollar bill out of his pocket and gave it to the boy. Huck took it and jammed it into his pocket. He didn't seem surprised, or angry, or dejected even. There was only the unmistakable look of resignation. He was on his own, just like he'd always expected, twenty bucks in his pocket and beholden to nobody—it was, Ralph figured, about as good a start as any.

# *Status Zero*

THERE WAS BLOOD EVERYWHERE. IT HAD SPLATTERED ONTO THE YELLOW CURTAINS AND THE NEW BERBER carpet and dried into the little fibers so that he had to scrub with a wire brush. Skull fragments were lodged into the wall. He had to pry them out with pliers. Later he would have to smooth the wall out with plaster and paint over the cavities. He found bits of skull underneath the bed. He found brain tissue, the texture of beef jerky. These would be collected and then incinerated in a large furnace back at the office. Being the new guy, Max figured this would be his responsibility.

A middle-aged man, director of the local food bank and father of two, had shot himself with a recently purchased 9mm semi-automatic Beretta. He'd left a note. Officially, the cops weren't allowed to share that sort of information with Apex BioClean, Max's new employer, a crime-scene/suicide cleaning agency, though his co-workers said they almost always did. This one, it was rumored, had simply said, "I'm sorry—I can't provide for you any longer. Please contact Michael Thomas, our insurance agent, about collecting life insurance money. If they refuse to pay, hire a lawyer.

There's a two-year exclusion on suicide. Afterwards, they have to pay. I checked."

He couldn't imagine finding such a note, then finding his spouse with half her face missing. It made Max not feel so bad about his own circumstances. Such trauma made your problems all of a sudden feel trivial and unimportant. To remind him of this, he pocketed a piece of molar. It was just a shard really, only distinguishable from other bone fragments because of the tiny bit of silver filling that remained.

"Excuse me," a voice said behind him. "I didn't realize anyone would still be here." He looked up. The voice belonged to a teenage girl, probably fifteen or sixteen. She wore glasses much too large for her face and stood behind the half-opened door. He must've looked a bit frightening. He wore a hazmat suit, made of nitrile rubber and an aluminized shell.

"I'm sorry." He really didn't know what else to say. He was on all fours, brushing commercial-grade disinfectant soap into the stains her father had made.

"No. Don't be. I'll get out of your way."

She left him to his work, which took two hours more. When he was done, he gathered his supplies and exited. He found her sitting at the kitchen bar. She wasn't watching television or eating a bowl of cereal or reading a magazine. She sat staring at nothing, the blank look of someone whose vision had blurred, lost in thought. Max wouldn't have been surprised if she'd been sitting there the entire time he'd been working. He'd never lost anyone before. His grandparents were still alive. No cousin had died in a tragic car accident. A friend hadn't passed away unexpectedly while on a ski trip, perhaps a little tipsy before flying headfirst into a fir tree. He had no idea what that was like, to mourn someone.

She smiled when she noticed him. "Finished?" she asked.

He'd taken his mask off even though he wasn't supposed to; he still carried human remains. "Yes," he said.

"My name's Alice, by the way," she said as if they'd bumped into each other twice in one day, two strangers, under normal, though improbable, circumstances.

"Max," he said.

"You been doing this long, Max?" she asked.

"My first job by myself, actually."

"They let you do this sort of thing by yourself?"

"We're shorthanded."

"I see."

An awkward silence followed.

"Don't worry," she said. "I won't tell anyone."

"I'm sorry?"

She pointed to his pocket. "I saw you pocket part of my dad." He froze. He could feel himself turn pale in embarrassment. "Don't worry," she repeated. "I'm not going to tell anyone."

"I'm so sorry."

"Stop."

"Really, I—"

"It's okay. Honest."

Without knowing what to say, he excused himself and began packing the biomaterial and cleaning supplies into the van.

Through the bay window, he could see Alice watching him, her head cocked and turned, reminding him of an ostrich. She was studying him, like a scientist might a newly discovered species. In his hurry to leave, he hadn't properly closed the container holding the remains of the deceased, and as he threw the supplies into the back of the van, the container tipped over and spilled dried gray matter. He should've immediately disposed of the remains and de-contaminated the van, but he didn't, uncomfortable under Alice's close scrutiny.

THE NICKNAMES BEGAN ALMOST AS soon as he'd unpacked his last box: Boomerang Boy, The Renter, Maxy the Moocher. He tried to laugh alongside his father—he was, after all, trying to make the best of the situation. Economics degree in hand, he'd been unable to find work for six months after graduating and had, embarrassingly enough, been evicted from his one-bedroom apartment, forced to return to his parents' home to sleep in his childhood bedroom. It was humiliating. When he thought about it, which was most of the time, he couldn't help but want to hide indefinitely.

It became worse during his father's monthly barbecue, where the old man would invite his schmoozer friends over to eat pulled pork, drink beer, and place wagers on his manicured putting green tucked away in the corner of their backyard. His father was a commercial lender at a privately held bank specializing in real estate development, so there was a lot of the proverbial influential class of Oklahoma City present, semi-drunk and one-upping each other. They should be able to get Max a job, but that would, his father maintained, be unethical, not to mention nepotistic. They were his clients after all. Not friends. Max couldn't help but notice, however, how they drank his father's beers like friends.

Max was expected to schmooze alongside his father anyway, drinking American lager and missing short putts on purpose. At this moment, he was holding the pin for his father, who'd wagered over $300 on a game of LAFFER, a take on basketball's HORSE but named after the notorious economist, Arthur Laffer. Laffer devised the Laffer curve, a hypothetical representation of the relationship between tax rates and tax revenues, arguing that the higher the rate, the less the government would reap. Basically, one contestant in the game would putt from a spot of his choice, and if he sank it, then his challenger would have to sink the same putt. If the challenger missed, then he obtained a letter in LAFFER. The first one whose letters spelled Mr. Laffer's surname in its entirety lost. Max's father, Aubrey, led Mr. Dillard, a used-car salesman turned real estate developer, E to second F. Max had recently turned in resumes to both Mr. Dillard's finance company, which funded his buy-here, pay-here car dealership, and to the development company. He hadn't received a call back on either.

It was Mr. Dillard's shot. He lined up an eight-footer on the east side of the green, which faced an uphill grade with a right-to-left slant of approximately four degrees, a relatively easy shot for a sober person. He took a few practice swings and then inched up to the ball. Except for the occasional sip from a beer, the backyard was quiet. Mr. Dillard's tongue hung limply from his lips in concentration. He swung. The ball followed the grade beautifully, curving slightly towards the pin. Max raised it, but the ball lipped out and swung eight inches or so from the cup.

"Always hung a little to the left, hasn't it, Pickle?" Aubrey said, a bad nickname he had for Mr. Dillard. Dill pickle. Get it?

"Long and lanky," Mr. Dillard said. "As always."

It was now Aubrey's shot. He circled the cup, trying to find the most difficult shot he could make. Max's father had always been a golfer, a passion he'd tried to pass down to Max, though it never really took. Max remembered many nights out here practicing, his father crouched like a catcher as he coached Max on how to keep his shoulders square, how to keep his line of vision straight down the club, and how to minimize motion in the putting stroke. Max never thought his father was living vicariously through him, goading him into youth tournaments in order to fulfill his own PGA fantasies. Mostly, Max considered his pushing as a means to build a connection, find some hobby that bonded them together, a thing just their own. By the time Max reached his teenage years, though, he informed his father he no longer wished to golf. It wasn't that he hated golfing *per se*, but he got tired of losing week in and week out, routinely missing the cut and having to stay home on Sundays and listen to his father's condolences. You'll get 'em next time. Just keep your head up. You're due for a win. He was absolutely sure of it. That weekend, the clubs went up into the attic, not to come down again until his fraternity brothers and he would get drunk on the front nine when they should've been studying for midterms. Now, at the barbecue, Aubrey focused on his own shot, a snaking fourteen-footer, as Max fought back the urge to tell him to square up his shoulders and quit wobbling so much. It wasn't needed, though. He sank it with a satisfying plunk into the bottom of the cup.

"You always wait until I get a good buzz going," Mr. Dillard said. "It's the only way you can win." Mr. Dillard lined up the same shot as Aubrey'd made. If he missed, he would lose. Unhappy with how it looked, he crouched and shut one eye, trying to discern the grade and angle needed. "Got any tips?" he asked Max.

"I'm sorry, sir?"

"Tips. I'm sure you know this green. Got any advice so I don't lose to your old man?"

"No. I'm sorry."

"None at all?"

"Don't miss?"

"I see." Mr. Dillard twirled the putter and then dropped it accidentally on the green, moving the ball. After fumbling it a few times, he placed it back where it needed to go and picked up the putter. "Perhaps you just don't have enough vested in the shot. Here." He held the handle out for Max to take. "You shoot."

"I don't think that would be wise, sir."

"And why's that?"

"I'm not very good."

"Okay. Okay. Let's make it a little interesting, then. You sink the putt, and I'll hire you on."

"Really?"

"Absolutely."

Max checked the others' faces, Aubrey's especially, to see if they believed Mr. Dillard. They all looked on, interested in the outcome, none with a look of uncertainty.

"I sink the putt, and you'll give me a job?"

"Why not?"

Max had a multitude of why nots. Fiscal responsibility. Efficient operations. Profit maximization theory. Marginal cost equals marginal revenue. They were in a recession, for Christ's sake, or at least GDP growth was minimal enough to stall the recovery. Offering jobs on a drunken whim didn't seem prudent. Downright foolish actually.

"Okay. Sure. I'll shoot."

Mr. Dillard rubbed his hands together in excitement. "Good. Great. Now things are getting interesting."

Max took the putter and lined up the shot the best he could. He could feel his father and his friends watching him. It was funny—he considered himself an adult now, despite his living conditions, but he couldn't help but feel like he was a child again, performing under his father's scrutiny. With it came the unshakeable desire to please him. It made Max ashamed in a way, and he hoped they were too drunk to notice his cheeks turning red.

With a smooth motion he reared back the head, his arms and shoulders still, allowing his torso to do the work, and struck the ball. It was a clean shot. The ball moved well at a good speed and followed the sloping green toward the cup. It looked like it was going to go in. It really did. In a collective hush, he could hear all his father's friends suck in one large breath, but then release it in a plume of hot wind as the ball lipped the edge and rolled mere inches from the cup.

HE SAW HER EVERY MORNING afterward. She would wait in the park opposite Apex BioClean's offices, and she would be there when he returned the van in the evening. She wasn't trying to hide by any means—she sat on a park bench clearly facing the front of the building. She looked out of place there. Despite the triple-digit heat, she wore an oversized sweatshirt and picked dandelion fuzz from her hair. A bicycle lay on its side at her feet. Books were stacked neatly next to her, though Max never saw her actually read one. It was like she was on a stakeout but wanted the suspect to know she was onto him. She obviously wanted to talk to him, but she didn't for a while. The other guys began to notice and make snide comments. Probably a Goth girl. A necrophile. A necromancer. Finally, after a week, she approached.

It was awkward for sure. She hugged a book to her chest, some paperback, her hands hidden underneath her sleeves.

"Hey," she said.

"Hey." Max didn't know what to do or say. He still had her father's tooth. He kept it with him actually, for reasons he couldn't articulate. A memento from his first job, he supposed, something that made him uncomfortable but that he couldn't bring himself to dispose of either. It fascinated him in a way, like how a sore on the inside of a cheek could, tonguing it despite the pain. "What're you doing here?"

"Can I ask you a question?"

"Sure."

She motioned toward Max's coworkers. "In private?"

Max led her to his van, opened the door for her, and helped her climb in. She was shorter than he remembered. Her feet barely touched the floor.

"Thanks," she said. "Those guys were kind of giving me the creeps."

Max nodded. "They tend to do that," he said, although he wasn't sure why. She was the one who'd been stalking their office. "What can I do for you?"

She leafed through the pages of the book she had brought with her. It was a tattered copy of *Grimm's Fairy Tales*. An odd choice for a teenage girl, Max thought.

"I want you to take me with you."

"I'm sorry?"

"On your next job. I want to go with you."

"I don't think I can do that."

"I'll stay out of your way. I promise. I just want to see."

She had a pensive quality to her. It gave her the air of a much older woman, perhaps the result of her father's death. He'd looked at pictures of her when he'd been alone in her house. He would've described her as baby faced. She still had the chubby cheeks and glittering eyes. She was the type of person who smiled with her entire body. But now she brooded. Her once-smooth features had been etched with lines of concern. Her posture had deteriorated into a slump.

"No, I mean, it's not up to me. It's against company policy."

"It won't be a big deal. I promise."

"I could lose my job."

"How about this," she said. "Take me with you, and I won't tell anybody that you took my father's tooth."

There it was. Blackmail. What else could he do?

The first job was on the northwestern side of town, not far from Max's house. In this part of the city, affluent neighborhoods abutted more blue-collar ones. Expansive green lawns gave way to Oklahoma's trademark red clay. When he'd been assigned the job, Max had assumed it would be in the more working-class neighborhood, but it wasn't. It was in Nichols Hills, one of the more prominent divisions in the city. Oilmen lived there. Bankers and attorneys and entrepreneurs. The house in question was owned by a doctor. Apparently, he'd snapped and was found cradling his lifeless son in his arms. He'd stabbed the boy thirty-four times in the torso, neck, and face. When the police found him, he kept repeating that the devil was in the boy, that he had to do it, he didn't have any other choice. The news had already gone national. Backgrounds and histories were dug up. The doctor had had psychological problems in the past. Twice he'd been institutionalized for depression and suicidal tendencies, once while in medical school and again during the first year of his residency. Lately he'd been under a lot of stress, his wife had said, due to an IRS audit of his practice. He went off his medication apparently, thinking he might sleep better.

It had happened in the kitchen. Blood stained the tile floor.

It hadn't stained the way spilt barbecue sauce would, just a slight film that could be scraped off. The blood had coagulated into a hard rubbery substance like the texture of a petri dish. Handprints painted cupboards. Small footprints inked the baseboard where the little boy had fought for survival. It was the most difficult thing Max had ever had to do, clean the site where a child had been murdered.

Alice did as she'd said she would; she stayed out of his way. While he scrubbed grout, she stayed in the breakfast nook, sitting with a paper pad in her lap, drawing the scene. Every once in a while she would ask Max to hold that spot for a second, she liked how the light caught the red and soap together. She showed him her work as she progressed. It wasn't very good. She tried a surrealistic approach, reminiscent of a Dali. Proportions were hyperbolic. Max appeared much larger than the stain he cleaned, the refraction of the light shot into a hinged rainbow like on the *Dark Side of the Moon* album cover. It gave the whole scene a comic quality to it, trivializing what had happened.

They continued on this way for the remainder of the day and for several days thereafter. She would wait in the park for him every morning, and he would pick her up a little ways down the street. He would clean, and she would draw. They would engage in small talk. It was almost like they were an old married couple, sentenced to talk about the trivial because they'd exhausted all that they had to say to one another. Soon Max became comfortable with this arrangement. He even started to look forward to it, the way an old married man might. He had his routine. He had his morning coffee, his newspaper, his work, and his wife. He had it all while he cleaned up the bloodied messes left by those around him.

HE STILL WENT ON INTERVIEWS. They were all for entry-level jobs. Some were in the oil and gas industry as a project analyst, scouring over geological surveys and cash-flow projections. Others were at Boeing where he would crunch raw material and labor costs. Still more at banks in operations departments, doing data entry and document prep. Entry level had a different meaning, he found out, than he'd been told at the career services department at school. Entry level now meant a minimum of two years' experience. This was a troubling thought. He needed experience to get an entry-level position. He needed the entry-level position to get experience.

It was supposed to be getting easier, wasn't it? The unemployment rate was falling, after all.

That didn't mean anything, though. The unemployment rate was calculated by dividing the number of unemployed over all potential workers. People who were no longer looking for work, however, and people like Max, recent graduates who weren't in education and had not previously held a professional job, were not considered either employed or unemployed. He was a non-person. He was, as the government deemed him, status zero. Ultimately, when it came right down to it, he felt lied to.

The woman interviewing him seemed to be lying to him, too. She had an office in the back of Coppermark Bank whose walls were made of glass and whose desk had business cards on it emblazoned with the words "Assistant Vice President." Her skin had grayed and looked weathered. It appeared she had drunk too much coffee; her eyebrow twitched as if being shocked by a low amount of electricity.

She asked questions that seemed scripted. Where do you see yourself in five years? What are your greatest strengths? Your weaknesses? What type of experience do you have? What type of loan documentation knowledge do you possess? What are you currently doing? Do you like that? Do you have reliable transportation? The job requires long periods of sitting and staring at a computer monitor, would that interest you? How fast is your ten-key? What days would you be available to work?

He took a personality test and an aptitude test. He performed basic algebra and answered logical questions such as if all As are Bs and all Bs are Cs but not all Cs are Bs, are all Cs As?

No, he answered. No, they are not.

After her questioning, she opened herself up to interrogation. Max himself relied upon a script given to him by a counselor at school. Base salary? Reasonable. Bonuses? Based on profits. Annually? Yes. Vacation time? Two weeks. Student loan reimbursement? No. These were mere formalities. He wouldn't get the job. He could tell by her dry, monotone voice and clipped answers, the way she sat on the edge of her seat, as if waiting to show him the door.

She thanked him for his time, and he for hers. They shook hands. She smiled and so did he. He took a card although he knew it to be worthless and placed it into his pocket. He kept his hand there as he exited and only took it out again after he heard the click of her door latching into place.

THEY WENT TO A REDHAWKS baseball game, the AAA affiliate of the Houston Astros. His father ordered a beer and a hot dog with sauerkraut, and Max a beer and peanuts. It was fall, and the team was sixteen games out of first, no chance of making the playoffs. The players didn't even care anymore. They lobbed the ball to one another and jogged to first. After a long and grueling season, Max couldn't blame them. They were hurt and tired and the games didn't mean anything. All they wanted was to earn their paychecks and go home. A sentiment Max could relate to.

Max listened to his father explain the game as if he'd never been to a baseball game before. He demystified the importance of the rosin bag in pitch control, the shift bunt defense, and the puzzling infield fly rule. Stalling tactics. Max could always tell when his father was about to broach a subject he didn't wish to. He looked like a pizza boy standing on a stoop, awaiting a tip that wouldn't come. Then he said, without the slightest bit of confidence, "You know, your mother and I have been talking."

"Uh-huh," Max said, a piece of peanut skin annoyingly stuck to his bottom lip.

"Let me predicate this by saying that we're glad you're living with us. We are. It's like old times."

Max didn't say anything. He and his father sat behind the third base dugout, and a group of teenagers behind them berated the third base coach. "MahOOooooney," they yelled. "You're full of balOOOoooney." They slurred their words and smelled of cheap beer. High school kids, more than likely, who had a former classmate working the beer stand or had fake IDs. They laughed and high-fived and cajoled. Max remembered having that sort of fun. He remembered right before graduation, he and his fraternity brothers had stolen a goat at a local petting zoo and got it drunk on Pabst and let it loose in the student union. It shat everywhere. It was the last time Max remembered laughing so hard he could hardly breathe.

"We just want to make sure that you're happy."

"I'm happy."

"Are you?"

The batter hit a foul groundball. Mahoney bent over to attempt to field it, but the ball kicked off his hands. The kids behind Max stood up and cupped their mouths. "Hey, Mahoney! Nice boot, cowboy! You couldn't catch a cold naked and wet in Canada!"

"Yes. I'm happy," Max said.

"Can you believe these kids?" Max's father pointed his thumb behind them. "Belligerent little shits."

Another time he and his friends had set an old couch on fire with roman candles and lighter fluid. He'd gone to Mardi Gras and ate so much crawfish that he'd puked the color and consistency of old tomato soup. A strange girl at a Bela Fleck and the Flecktones concert had felt him up when she'd passed him a joint. He missed that.

"I wish I wasn't living at home. Wish I had a job where I didn't clean up dead people."

The teenagers started heckling louder. I've seen better movement in a bedpan, they said. Hey two-four, your mom's a whore,
they said. On and on. MahOOooney. MahOOooney.

"Where are their parents, for Christ's sake? Or security?"

"It gets to you, you know? You start questioning yourself."

MahOOOoney. MahOOoney. MahOOOooney. He'd ig-
nored the kids' taunts up until this point. After they called his
mother a whore, though, Mahoney glanced up into the stands every few pitches or so. There was a hurt expression underneath his
hat brim. He looked lonely. He looked like a man who desperately
missed his mother.

"That's sort of what we wanted to talk to you about. Your
mother and I. We think it'd be best for everyone if you found your
own place."

"Like the other day. I stole a tooth from work. Some dead
guy's tooth. Who does that?"

"We'd help you out of course. We could pay your security de-
posit and first and last month's rent. You're making good money
now. Like twelve bucks an hour, right?"

There was a shot into the left-center gap, a real rocket that
sounded like a tree being struck by an axe. The batter rounded
first and picked up speed. He was a tall, gaunt man whose joints
seemed to jab in the air like a Bowflex machine. The ball rico-
cheted off the wall at a weird angle and shot past the left fielder.

"And now the guy's daughter is following me around! Like
she's fueling some weird curiosity about death now that her dad

shot his face off or maybe she has a crush on me. I don't know. But I can't tell her to stop. Not now. Not after what I did."

The runner rounded second and was approaching third. The left fielder bobbled the ball, and Mahoney was waving the runner to run home and score. All the while the kids were badgering this poor man who was only trying to do his job. MahOOoooney. You big, fat phOOooony.

"You're an adult now, son. I guess what I'm saying is that we want you out by the end of the month."

As the runner rounded third, he took a bad angle and looped a little further than Mahoney, who hugged the line too closely, expected. The runner ended up smashing into Mahoney, and the collision toppled Mahoney end over end. The defense finally re-layed the ball into the infield and tagged the runner out as he lay on the ground, rolling around in pain. Mahoney was motionless. The teenage kids laughed and laughed and laughed. You idiot, they said. You retard! Can't you do anything right?

"Shut up!" Max turned and yelled at the stunned kids. "Shut up, shut up, shut up!"

The trainer jumped from the dugout and raced out to the injured Mahoney. For a few seconds, the entire stadium was quiet. No one chomped on sunflower seeds or clapped their hands or whooped a cheer for the home team. There wasn't even a breeze. There was just a collective hush, shared by a few hundred people, and Max reveled in it; finally, a moment to collect his thoughts. But then it was broken, the silence, with a resounding taunt.

MahOOoooney.

THE SEX WASN'T PLANNED. HE hadn't gone to work that day wanting to touch her. The night before he hadn't dreamt of her. She didn't appear in fantasies so vivid he could taste the salt of her. After work he often forgot about her, worried about other things. During work she was a mere creature comfort, something outside the horror he had to face.

It was the final job of the day—this one had been an accident. A woman had been cleaning a shotgun not knowing it was loaded. At some point, she pulled the trigger and shot herself in the face. It was double-barreled, the gun, and caused a lot of damage. Alice found a piece of mandible behind the recliner, covered in tissue and curved like a mouth guard.

"It sort of reminds me of Halloween, you know. Those props you find in a haunted house. Like you wouldn't even know it was real unless you *knew* knew. Know what I mean?" she said.

He did.

"All this stuff does. Once you get used to the smell, you kind of get used to all of it," she continued. "You get desensitized in a way. You lose all sense of how macabre all this shit is. Like a funeral home director. Or a soldier."

"It still drags on you, though."

She shrugged. "I guess." She flicked graphite from her pad of paper. She was drawing the mandible. She had it sitting on the dining room table as if it were a vase of flowers.

He cleaned the dried blood from the walls. The paint chipped as he scrubbed, and he would have to prime and repaint before the tenants returned. He dislodged shot pellets from the drywall.

"Is it weird that this sort of stuff kind of turns me on?" she said.

He stopped cleaning and turned to her. She hadn't moved much. She sat like a behaved student might, her knees and heels touching, back straight, a pad of paper on her legs. He thought of a schoolgirl fantasy, and it made him nauseated. He'd always been embarrassed by the act of sex. The few times he had done it, he did so with the lights switched off and with girls he knew from class. Afterward, he wouldn't know how to act, and they, sensing his discomfort, would soon stop calling or coming by his dorm room. When he saw them in econometrics or in derivatives and options securities, he would act like nothing had happened, and he sensed that they were laughing behind his back.

This feeling of embarrassment returned to him like the memory of a friend he'd wronged years ago might, out of the blue and coupled with a feeling of shame. They both sat staring at each other for quite a while after she said this, she, he thought, expecting him to make a move and him frozen in anxiety. It was like he could actually feel the lining in his stomach walls thin.

It wasn't there that they had sex, but later, in the back of the van as he packed his cleaning supplies and the human remains. Alice made the first move. Max pushed in the buckets of commercial grade disinfectant soap, and when he turned around, she loomed but a few inches away. She paused right there as if asking if it was okay that she was so close. When he didn't object, she tiptoed up to kiss him. He leaned back against the van's bumper, his lips tight and unresponsive to hers, but he couldn't help but think how good she tasted. It was like sour grapes and popcorn and the comfort of no responsibilities.

HE DIDN'T RETURN TO WORK after that. He didn't call or resign or give two weeks' notice; he simply quit. His last paycheck would not be cashed, despite the company mailing it to him, and it would eventually be forgotten in some drawer. He tried to tell himself the reason was the work. Who could face that, day in and day out? Death and the sad survivors, their belongings forever scarred by what had transpired there. And then that smell. He couldn't get it off of him at night. He would shower as soon as he returned to his parents' house, and he would scrub and scrub and scrub, but it wouldn't come off of him. It followed him everywhere, like an old dog would, mere days from death itself. After awhile, he even started believing that that was the case, that it was the work and not what he had done to Alice that drove him to quit.

He didn't tell his father. In the mornings they would have coffee together. His father would ask him rhetorical questions about the Fed's quantitative easing policy or if he should refinance his house because interest rates were so low. They would make plans to go see a basketball game or take a vacation to Dallas and intentionally ignore the fact Max hadn't moved out yet. Then they would say their goodbyes, leaving the house at the same time, and both wouldn't get home until much later when they would be too tired to spend any time with each other.

Max spent his days simply walking around town, already having given up on responding to want ads. He would stop in diners and eat a piece of pie and leave a generous tip since it wasn't his money—it was his parents'—and then catch an exhibit on the theory of relativity at the Omniplex and then a matinee at the dollar theater to see last year's big summer blockbusters. When it was too cold or if the wind was too harsh, he would duck into coffee shops and nurse a cup of coffee as he stared at the passing cars. He enjoyed the solitude during these outings. He didn't feel the need to speak to anyone or explain himself. Sometimes he would try to go the whole day without uttering a word.

It was on a day like this that he found himself in front of the high school, his alma mater. His hands were tucked into his pockets. He clutched Alice's father's tooth and rubbed it between his fingertips. It felt odd in his hands, almost like plastic. He wandered around campus for a while. He walked the track. He circled the parking lot. He read the marquee at the auditorium. Finally, he simply walked in. It looked much like it had when he'd been a student there. The linoleum floors. Old steel lockers. Pep rally banners made from cardstock and glitter paint. It even smelled the same, like disinfectant and tater tots. The halls were empty. No kids were walking to the office or the bathroom. It was odd, like a ghost town. He even peeked his head into a classroom. No one was in there.

He sat at a desk and tried to remember if he'd had this classroom for government or English. It was a science classroom now. A periodic table of the elements covered most of the eastern wall. Microscopes lined lab tables behind the desks. There were gas nozzles and an eye washing station. He wrote on the blackboard the only scientific formula he could remember, $E = mc^2$, and then left.

He found everyone in the gymnasium. On the court were the football team and the cheerleaders. The band played the school fight song as the student body all stood and cheered. Banners waved. Everyone clapped in unison. It made Max feel nostalgic in a way he hadn't in years.

After a few seconds in the doorway, a man wearing a suit approached him. Max remembered him; it was Mr. Byers, the assistant principal. Max expected him to ask what he was doing there. Unannounced visitors were rarely welcomed onto school campuses, even if they were alumni. Instead, he asked Max where he'd been.

Confused, Max said, "I'm sorry?"

"Get back in the stands," he said.

Mr. Byers thought Max was a student. For a moment, Max considered correcting him and then leaving, but he decided not to. Instead, he found an open seat on the front row between two students. They didn't even give him a second glance as he began to clap alongside them. They thought he was supposed to be there just like Mr. Byers did. It was calming in a way. He belonged someplace. He didn't have to think about his joblessness or lack of an apartment. He could simply get caught up in the revelry, blending into the cheering crowd, a single digit amid a long line of zeros.

# Everything's Fine

WHEN I WAS A CHILD, I TIED ROPES
AROUND MY LEGS. I TIED THEM AS TIGHT AS I COULD, UNTIL MY
skin turned pink, then red, then purple. I didn't lose feeling right
away—my legs tingled at first. They felt heavy, and when I tried
to move them, waves rushed through my body. They weren't pain-
ful, more uncomfortable, like placing your tongue on the end of a
9-volt battery. I could hardly stand the feeling when it was there,
but I missed it when it was gone. I tied my legs until I couldn't
feel my calves or my ankles or my toes, until they were just dead
weight. I tied the ropes so tight my legs were both a part of my
body and not a part of my body, so tight they felt disjointed from
the rest of me. It was comforting in a sense—it was like I could
detach myself from the world if I needed to.

After a while, the tissue became damaged. Capillaries burst.
During the day, my legs throbbed in pain. I walked with a limp,
and my parents worried. They took me to doctors, and when it
finally came out what I was doing, they took me to psychiatrists.
They removed the ropes from my room, but I found new ways.
I'd cut the power cords off of lamps and use those instead. When

those were taken away, I used the elastic in my underwear. I used the cords from the blinds and the bungee ties in the garage and basketball nets from the school. I used anything I could get my hands on.

One night, after tying off with a couple Hanes T-shirts, I decided to go for a walk. I wanted the wavelike sensation to shoot up my body until I couldn't take it any longer, and so I stood and used the wall to brace myself as I left my room. It was quiet in the house. It was about 1:00 a.m. and my parents had gone to sleep hours before. Downstairs, a kitchen light dimly illuminated the house, and I decided to get myself a glass of water. I turned toward the stairs, my legs wobbly underneath me, and as I passed the third step, I stumbled and lost my balance. I tried to catch myself on the railing, but I couldn't, and I fell. Unable to raise my arms to brace myself, my face collided with a corner, and my nose snapped in two. I broke a rib and a wrist and tore a ligament in my elbow. I chipped one tooth and lost another. Contusions covered most of my body, and I burned and throbbed.

But the pain was only from the waist up, my legs devoid of serious injury. There was just that wavelike sensation as I regained feeling. It was slow at first. Blood filled my mouth, and I had to spit so I wouldn't choke. I wiggled my toes, but there wasn't any pain. I next moved my ankles, and then my calves, bending at the knees. I put a little pressure on them, not standing right away, but slowly, until I was on both feet again, and as I took my first step I realized I was fine—just fine.

I worked at Rosewood Medical Center for the Severely Disabled in The Village. A former suburb of Oklahoma City, it was built by oil-company middle managers in the fifties and sixties. It had long since been annexed by the city, the middle managers having all moved further way from the central business district, replaced now by a more diverse set of wage earners: janitors and gas station attendants and truck drivers and young professionals. The streets smelled of bacon and burgers and the dog food factory a few miles away. The medical center itself was quiet and lonely. That may be why I liked it so much—I could go an entire day without speaking to anyone, and it wouldn't arouse a single person's suspicions.

My job was to keep things calm and neat and orderly. Most of my days were spent cleaning bedpans, laundering sheets, and mopping floors. I changed the TV channel if the programming became too violent or loud or if the colors were too sharp or bright. I washed dishes after lunchtime and gave sponge baths. The doctor who managed Rosewood was a big proponent of touching. He wanted us to touch the patients as much as possible. He asked us to pat the patients' shoulders or to hug them. We held hands and ran our fingers through their hair. As often as we could, we were to let them know we were near, and that we cared.

One patient was named Harry Humboldt. A middle-aged Huntington's disease victim, most of the time it seemed he didn't know much of what was going on around him. His head bobbed and his muscles tensed, but he still had some cognitive abilities—if you touched his shoulder, his head jerked in your direction, and his eyes softened, and his tongue hung from the corner of his mouth. He knew when I was there, and I think he was appreciative of my company. I enjoyed spending time with him as well. Oftentimes I found myself confessing my sins to him as if he were a priest, how I'd sat on my hand for an entire hour, until my circulation had been cut off for so long my fingers were the color of plums. I told him how I sometimes took the entirety of a take-a-penny, leave-a-penny jar and dumped the contents into my purse. I told him how I'd wait at a stoplight until it turned red so the guy behind me couldn't cross, and the entire time Harry listened to me with his soft eyes, and I knew deep down he didn't judge me.

I was intimate with Harry once per week. The act itself usually lasted no more than a minute or two, but the whole process was enacted with dignity and respect and without judgment—just a man experiencing the intimacy and touch of another human being. I lay next to him as I rubbed his penis, and he stared straight ahead and I'd rest my head on his shoulder. He always had this immense amount of pleasure on his face. He smiled, the only time I could say with confidence he did, and when he reached orgasm, his head slumped to his chest. Afterwards, I cleaned him up and left him alone for a few moments with his thoughts. Then I'd call an orderly, and watch as they laid him down to rest.

HARRY'S BROTHER FRANK VISITED AT least three times a week. Frank was older, in those indeterminate years between middle-age and senior citizenship. He always came alone, ate a club sandwich, and hardly said a word. They watched *The Price is Right* and *Family Feud* and *Jeopardy* together, Frank every once in a while exclaiming, "What is *Back to the Future*," or "$10,250," depending on the show. While visiting, I tried to stay out of the room, only peering in every so often to check Harry's health monitors, make sure his water cup was full, or if his colostomy bag needed changing. When I was in the room, Frank stared at me the way men have since I was eleven years old, with a mixture of lust and apathy.

At first, I wasn't attracted to Frank, but I was interested in him. To be so devoted to his brother, he had to have some level of goodness in him. He also seemed so lonely, and in that I found comfort—I found something I recognized—but it was Gloria, a talkative woman I'd worked with for several years, who first broached the subject of Frank and I going out. Frank was standing at the entrance signing the check-in sheet, and I was behind the reception area logging the most recent bathroom cleaning, when she spoke.

"You're single, right?" Gloria asked, pointing first at me and then at Frank. "You two should date."

It wasn't so much we said yes—it was just neither one of us said no.

For our first date, Frank took me to an outdoor movie at the botanical gardens—Meg Ryan and Tom Hanks in *Sleepless in Seattle*—so we could watch his ex-wife. She sat five rows in front of us with her new family, a middle-aged husband and twin teenage daughters. They weren't so much new, really. Frank and she, Tina was her name, were married for only six months twenty years ago, but he followed her most every night.

"I just like to see her happy," he said.

As it turned out, I liked seeing her happy, too. She was elegant and long-necked and her shoulders reminded me of a bowstring pulled taut. She had the longest fingers I had ever seen, and her life reminded me of a Crate & Barrel catalogue, filled with happy, smiling memories and sun-kissed afternoons and pumpkin spice scented kitchens. Her life was enviable in a way I didn't know existed in real life—it was like I wanted to get close enough to smell her.

At the movies, she twined her long fingers in her two beautiful daughters' hair. When she laughed, she laughed with her whole body. When she cried, she did so with aplomb, and without abasement. It was like she filled up all the space around her. She filled up the botanical gardens. She filled up the screen. She filled up the sky and the city and me, too. I was filled with so much joy I didn't know what to do with myself, and so I grabbed Frank's hand and I squeezed and he squeezed and, for a time, we were happy.

That night, we made love. He lay on top of me and he groaned and it was over quickly. Afterwards, he ate a bowl of Raisin Bran. He poured sugar over the flakes and let it soak in the milk for a good long while. He savored every bite, moaning each time he swallowed the same way he had when he'd been inside me.

Our relationship progressed from there. Each night we watched his ex-wife and her family. We followed them to dance recitals and to softball games, and we'd hide near their property and watch them enjoy a nightcap next to their pool. We watched them shop for groceries or a new car or take a family trip to the zoo, jumping when the chimpanzees pounded against their glass enclosures. We watched them cook dinner and take family photographs and feed their pugs and order around the Mexicans who mowed their lawn, and all the while Frank held me close and I rubbed my face against his chin stubble.

"How long have you been watching them?" I asked.

"About ten years," Frank said.

"When's the last time you spoke to her?"

"When she told me she was leaving me."

"And they don't know you watch?"

He shook his head. "They don't pay enough attention."

And things were good, so good after a while we sometimes didn't have to watch his ex-wife. We caught a movie or grabbed a bite to eat—we did normal things, went on normal dates, and had normal sex, almost to the point we convinced ourselves we were normal. Most nights passed without us saying more than three or four sentences to each other, but that was okay—preferable, in fact. He stayed over at my place and I at his. We even had emergency toothbrushes. For a time, we convinced ourselves it could last forever.

I even took him to meet my parents. We went to my childhood home for dinner, and Mom baked us a casserole and Dad served the good whiskey and we sat around the dining room table as a family for the first time in more than a decade. It had been a while since I'd been home, but the place still smelled the same, like dill pickles and coffee creamer. Mom interrogated Frank, asking about his job and how we'd met and his family, and Frank offered her short, clipped answers: taxidermist, visiting his brother, only the brother was left. Dad eyed Frank, but didn't ask questions, judging and inventorying, casting aspersions and jumping to conclusions. After dinner, Mom and I did the dishes while Frank and my father bonded over a single malt. Interesting, is what my mother called him.

"And you're happy with him?" she asked.

I told her I was.

"Well," she said. "As long as you're not hurting yourself."

Frank and I left and didn't return, opting instead to spend our nights watching Tina and her husband because everything was much better that way. We were happier watching Tina get her nails done or shopping for a new Christmas tree or waiting to get her oil changed. As we watched, we talked about the future. We talked about Harry and us moving in together and how we'd be happy as Tina fought with her family over the TV remote. After she kissed her daughters good night, Frank and I made love, and he lay on top so I could feel his weight bearing down upon me.

After a while, though, Tina's husband ruined everything. He left early in the morning and returned late in the evening, his absence conspicuous on the weekends, when she and her daughters hung out in the backyard. He didn't come home some nights, not returning until the morning, zigzagging as he made his way to the front door. He missed a birthday and once even passed out in the front yard. It was something that built up over time, this tension he caused, starting out as a slight tingle, much like when I'd tie my legs until they went numb, but soon it grew in intensity until it seemed like electricity swimming through the air. I could feel it from our vantage point in the woods, hunkered down with binoculars. In Tina's face was this sadness, and hurt, and angst, and it affected Frank and me, too. When she was sad, we no longer touched, and every time I reached for his hand or he mine, we moved our hands away.

Eventually, Tina confronted her husband. They were in the kitchen, and Frank and I were in our usual spot along the tree line, watching. The kids were in their rooms upstairs, and we could see the whole family through their windows. It was early on Sunday and the back of the house faced the east and the morning light cast the house in orange. It was like watching a play, but with the actors ignorant of their audience's presence.

At first, we didn't know they were fighting. They simply stood there. Through our binoculars, we could see their words were pointed and with focus, consonants snapped off the tongue, but their movements weren't animated, their necks not strained from yelling. I suppose they were trying to keep their voices low so as not to arouse the suspicions of their daughters upstairs. And it appeared they were succeeding. The girls watched television diligently, some high school drama flashing on the screen.

Back downstairs the fight progressed. The husband ran his hands down his face, pulling at his cheeks, and he frowned and puckered his mouth like he was eating something sour. Tina, however, wouldn't stop talking. I tried to read her lips as she spoke, but it was difficult. Her accusations were adamant, her lips forming around the words like helium trapped in a balloon. *How could you?* It looked like she said. *How could you? How could you? How could you?*

And then he slapped her. He slapped her one, and he slapped her hard. I jumped and Frank jumped, and Tina just stared at her husband in disbelief. She didn't have to say it this time—everyone was thinking it: *How could you?*

FRANK AND I STOPPED SEEING each other. It wasn't something demarcated or defined. We didn't break up; he just stopped showing up when I got off work. He stopped taking me to watch Tina. He stopped taking me to the movies or staying at my place or eating my cereal. He even stopped visiting his brother. I wasn't sure if Harry even noticed, however—our days still filled with the same routine. First thing in the morning, I changed his colostomy bag. I wheeled him down the hall and gave him a bath and together we picked out the clothes he'd wear. That day, we selected a Hawaiian shirt with large pink flowers on it.

We ate breakfast: yogurt and fruit puree. Harry always chewed with his mouth open and the sound it made comforted me. I then told him all I'd done the day before. I told him how I'd cut in line at the movie theater and pretended to not understand English when the patrons behind me complained. I told him how I shoplifted all the hand sanitizer from Walgreens and dumped the contents in the water fountain outside city hall. I told him how I moved a child's bike a street over to see how long it took the owner to locate it. I didn't, however, tell him how I missed his brother and how I wondered why he wasn't visiting anymore. I didn't tell him how I now watched Tina alone and hoped Frank would return, although he never did. I didn't tell him how I watched Tina's husband move out while the daughters sat on the front porch crying. I didn't tell him how unhappy Tina looked. I didn't tell him how she often sat downstairs on the couch alone for hours. I didn't tell him how when her daughters did talk to her, she stared past their heads with an unfocused gaze. I didn't tell him those things because he had enough to worry about without hearing my problems, too.

That afternoon, Harry and I went for a walk. It was windy and cold, so I put Harry in a jacket and wool beanie. I showed him the 7-Eleven that had been robbed the week before and the house where there'd been reports of dogfights. I even showed him Tina and her now ex-husband's house where she still lived with her two daughters. I showed him where they used to play horseshoes as a family and drink margaritas by their pool. I showed him where one of the pugs was buried and where the daughters hid their beer. I showed him all the secrets I knew, but Harry didn't seem to care, sniffling from the cold.

That night, I turned the heater up in his room and slowly took off his clothes. His body was rigid and pale and mostly just skin and bones, his legs and arms having atrophied over the years. I laid him down on his bed and warmed my hands over the heater, and then rubbed them up and down his body. I held him to let him know I was there, to let him know someone cared about him, that when he woke up and when he was scared and when he felt alone, he really wasn't. I made sure he felt safe and he felt loved, because he was, and everyone should feel that way every so often.

After a couple of minutes, the door unexpectedly opened. I was lying next to Harry in bed, and I didn't have time to move or to cover Harry up, and so Frank walked in and found me in bed with his brother's penis in my hand. I expected Frank to have some sort of reaction—to be angry, to be jealous, to turn and run away. But he didn't do anything like that. Instead, he just stood there. He just stood there and didn't have any sort of reaction at all.

HARRY MOVED OUT OF THE Rosewood Medical Center two days later. I wasn't told about the move, and I hadn't been there when it happened. I didn't actually find out about it until the following Monday when I returned to work. I put my lunch in the break room, poured myself a cup of coffee, enjoyed two or three sips, washed my hands, and then started my rounds. I always saved Harry for last so that he could sleep a little later, so I could spend a little more time with him, but when I opened his door, another man lay in Harry's bed. Another man's belongings decorated the walls. Another man's waste waited for me to clean. The realization that Harry was gone was a deflating one, a punctured tire losing air pressure.

The new man, a quadriplegic named Walter from Wisconsin, had been injured in a car accident. He and his wife had driven their Chevy to town to celebrate his seventy-eighth birthday, but Walter suffered a stroke on Second Street. Their sedan careened across the intersection and collided with the First State Bank at more than sixty miles per hour. Three died in the accident, two bank customers and Walter's wife, Shirley. His son placed Walter in here because he didn't know what else to do with him. The whole thing was tragic and senseless and over in just a few seconds.

I ended up leaving Rosewood myself, finding a new job working for an amusement park called Frontier City. I figured I needed a new scene, someplace not so lonely or sad, a place instead full of people, laughter, and the high-pitched shrill of a teenager's joy as she rode the loopty-loop. My job was to clean the grounds, continually crossing the park to pick up cigarette butts and sucker sticks and Gatorade bottles. Occasionally, I hosed down vomit from a ride or disinfected a bathroom stall after a guest with irritable bowels had tried one of the park's deep-fried offerings. Such things would bother most, but I grew accustomed to them.

It wasn't a bad job, though. I enjoyed it even. I enjoyed the feeling of being alone amid a legion of strangers. I enjoyed walking against the grain of an oncoming crowd. I enjoyed being able to feel it all around me, the people and the rides and the concrete under my feet. I enjoyed how the hose felt in my hand and the friction from my broom sweeping the pavement. I enjoyed the mist coming off the log ride and the late-evening sun warming my legs. Sometimes, I felt so much at once it was overwhelming, as if I was filling up to the point of bursting. Most of all, though, I enjoyed thinking Frank might be out in the crowd somewhere, and I couldn't find him because I wasn't paying enough attention.

# Brought To You By Anonymous

JUST AFTER DAWN, RUSTY AWOKE TO THE BUZZ OF A CHAINSAW. OUTSIDE, HE FOUND HIS NEXT-DOOR neighbor, Gil, hacking at the overgrown Pastuchov's ivy he'd planted a few years back. Gil waved the chainsaw about, sweeping it back and forth like a dizzy child trying to demolish a piñata. Soon, all of their neighbors had awoken. They came out in their robes, sipping coffee, wading through waist-high grass to see Gil going crazy. No one attempted to stop him, and with good cause—he looked deranged, like if you tried to reason with him, he'd slice you down as well.

Not that Rusty blamed him. The neighborhood looked wild. The entire city did. Left to its own devices, nature will overtake manmade structures. It will crumble concrete. It will shatter glass and warp shingles and weaken steel. It will rot wood and crumble asphalt. It will oxidize copper and turn iron into rust. It doesn't even take that long. Without regular maintenance, it's only a matter of weeks. Take grass for example; during a Midwestern spring, grass will grow approximately two feet each month.

It sounded impossible, but that was what had happened. Potholes on I-40 and the Broadway Extension formed quickly, filled in with weeds that punctured through the asphalt. Children's playgrounds around Hefner Lake turned unusable, pockmarked by moss and dandelions and hornets' nests. That was the worst—the insects. They swarmed everywhere: locusts and cicadas and beetles and cockroaches and spiders and flies and moths and mosquitoes.

The quickness of the city's transformation, however, was misleading. Rusty couldn't see the grass growing. He couldn't see rust spreading. That happened a little at a time, so that if you continuously peered at it, you'd swear there weren't any changes at all.

Not long after Gil took the chainsaw to his Post Oak, sirens sounded in the distance. Three police cruisers soon arrived, and out popped six cops, guns drawn, their badges gleaming. Gil didn't put up any fight, though. As soon as he noticed them, he killed the engine to the chainsaw and dropped it to the ground. The police drew carefully towards him, handcuffed him, and then holstered their weapons.

When Gil was placed in the back of the police cruiser, the onlookers retreated back into their houses to start their day.


DEBORAH AND RUSTY WERE AT the mall shopping for Riley's birthday. It was packed for a Thursday evening; teenagers milled around the food court, young parents pushed strollers filled with wild-eyed babies, middle-aged men tried on fleece vests, their wives puckering their lips in disapproval, and then there was them, completely lost as to what an eleven-year-old girl would want.

WHEN THEY'D ASKED HER IN previous weeks, she said, "I don't know. I have everything I need."

No use to a clueless parent.

They checked out new video games. Most of them seemed too violent for her age, shooting dinosaur-like aliens or beheading bloodthirsty zombies. She was too old for Build-A-Bear and Legos, not yet ready for jewelry or makeup. A clerk at a bookstore recommended the latest YA fiction, stories about teenage wizards and dystopian futures where children fought to the death, but Riley was already bookish and withdrawn—they didn't feel the need to exacerbate that part of her personality.

As they shopped, Rusty slurped on a fruit smoothie, and Deborah appeared to touch every item they passed. She groped jeans and skirts and watches and hats. Some pigeons had flown in through a broken skylight, and they circled overhead. Every few feet or so, some bird poop would be glued to a handrail, and Deborah would have to raise her hand for a few moments so as to avoid it.

"I just don't know what to make of it," Deborah said. "What kind of kid doesn't want anything for her birthday?"

"I know," Rusty said. "It's just so weird. When I was a kid, I had a list of things I wanted. New basketball shoes and a Ken Griffey, Jr. jersey or the new Mario Kart game or Teenage Mutant Ninja Turtle action figures."

"I collected fossils. Shark teeth and iguana bones. Anything creepy and crawly."

"You were a weird kid."

"Do you think something might be wrong with her? Some sort of anti-social behavior?"

"No," Rusty said. "No way. She's just shy."

"I don't know. She rarely goes over to friends' houses. That Rachel girl invites her over, and Cheryl. I've talked to their parents over the phone, but she has never invited anyone over to the house. Have you ever met *any* of her friends?"

He admitted that he had not.

"That's strange, isn't it? It has to be."

Rusty had noticed, and it did seem odd, though, he figured, it was way too premature to diagnose Riley as having some emotional problem. She could be going through puberty, her hormones creating irrational insecurities that would eventually ebb away. Perhaps she considered herself too mature for her peers at school. A little presumptuous, but nothing a little humility couldn't restrain. She just needed something, a spark, to ignite her interest in becoming sociable.

The tech store seemed promising. It bustled with kids, kids Riley's age. They surfed social networking sites and played Bejewelled and Fruit Ninja. There they found a helpful salesman, Tim. A young guy himself, he wore thick plastic glasses and tight jeans and the store's signature T-shirt that simply said "Genius" on the front.

"Can't miss," he said. He held up an iPad.

"Really?" Deborah asked.

"Absolutely," he said. "She can keep track of friends, socialize, study, read, play games, watch movies, listen to music. She will always be connected."

"I don't know," Deborah said. "She's still not really interacting with anyone. Not in the flesh anyway." She had been spearheading the get-Riley-more-social initiative, planning the birthday party, inviting all her classmates, hiring a band, and signing Riley up for extracurricular activities, dance and softball and acting classes. Each one Riley would go to without a fuss, but after the second or third time she would inform them she didn't want to return. Deborah would try to persuade Riley to stick with it, but Rusty would be the one who eventually relented, allowing her to withdraw back into her room. He knew it wasn't good parental practice to let his child quit everything, but he was working on it.

"We'll take it," he said.

THE DAY OF THE BIRTHDAY party, they found Riley sitting in the bay window, reading a book. There wasn't much of a view any more. Tall grass and vines blocked the street, casting a shadow in a place that had once glowed with natural light. This didn't seem to bother Riley, though. She didn't even look up when her parents entered the room.

"Hey there, sweetie," Deborah said. "What are you reading?"

"Nothing," she said.

"Don't you want to join your friends?" Rusty asked. "They're waiting on you."

She shrugged. "Sure." She lowered the book and stood to follow, but then stopped. "What happened with Mr. Lindsey?" she asked, meaning Gil. "I haven't seen him in a couple days."

Rusty had been expecting this. "Well," he said. "He did something against the rules, so the police came and arrested him."

"He broke the law?"

"Yes. He broke the law."

"But that seems silly," she said. "It's his tree. Why can't he cut it down?"

"Well, honey," Gil said. "It's against the law."

"I don't understand."

"Sometimes you just have to do what you're told whether it's silly or not."

"That's the stupidest thing I've ever heard."

"I know, sweetie. Sometimes life doesn't make sense. You'll learn that once you get older," he said, even though he had a hard time understanding it himself. Everyone had applauded the new legislation when it was passed, heralding it as a beautification milestone. It was thought that outlawing private citizens' ability to maintain their own personal property upkeep and outsourcing it to a single private contractor would reduce the emission of greenhouse gases, create a minimum standard of property maintenance, and allow consumers to keep more of their income, which, the theory went, would boost GDP growth through consumption. It passed through the legislature with bipartisan support with only a few naysayers. Everything had gone well at first. Dilapidated parts of the city experienced a rebirth. Older buildings were painted and repaired. Lawns were kept immaculate, green and trimmed. There was no trash floating along the streets, no graffiti defacing bridges. Developers, taking advantage of the beautification, expanded into areas that had once appeared risky. The economy surged. People seemed happier, jubilant even. But then eighteen months ago, three workers had been killed. They had been standing on the back of a trash truck when it malfunctioned, crunching them to death. The union went on strike, demanded higher wages, better benefits, and better equipment. The city couldn't meet their demands. Council members, in a legislative oversight, couldn't repeal the law without union consent, and the police, under direct threat from internal investigators, had to enforce the law and keep normal citizens from even mowing their grass. The result turned catastrophic as the city transformed into a wasteland. Buildings crumbled, streets were in disrepair, nature overwrought, wildlife clamored in, whitetails and bobcats and rattlesnakes. It seemed every day they would hear the crack of a rifle, echoing throughout the cityscape.

But how did you explain that to an eleven-year-old?

"But!" she protested. "But, but, but!"

"No buts. Go."

He pointed to where the other children were waiting in the den. They milled around for a while, chitchatted about things important to them—what new shoes Kevin Durant was wearing, a new album by some teenaged pop star Rusty'd never heard of, their new uber-evil history teacher. They played games, *balloon bull's-eye* and *who am I* and *flour cake*, all of which Deborah had discovered online. When it came time to open presents, Riley took center stage, wrapped boxes surrounding her like a fortress.

Riley ripped the paper off and tore at the cardboard boxes. She burst bubble wrap and dug through Styrofoam. But each time she came to the present, she looked disappointed. Inside would be a doll with braided blonde hair or an Easy Bake Oven or intricate Lego sets that depicted spaceships on the box. There was a bell to place on a bicycle's handlebars and movies about princesses and Trapper Keepers covered in glitter and pink. She held them in her hand, her posture deflated, her mouth puckered, and she would lay them to the side in a neat, uniform pile.

"Thank you," she mumbled to whomever gave her the gift.

Parents cast glances to one another, eyebrows arched in judgment. *Ungrateful little shit*, they seemed to say.

Soon, she got to the final gift, the gift from her parents. There was no way she would rebuff something so *cool*, so state of the art. By this time, Riley had lost most of her excitement, taking her time to dig her fingernails underneath the Scotch tape and pull it up slowly so as not to rip off part of the design. The iPad's box was white and modern and pristine. The device was pictured on the front, with its silver casing and sleek, black touchscreen. Rusty held his breath. He waited for it: a smile, a gasp, a jaw dropped. But they never came.

Riley blinked at it, then laid it with the rest.


THE FIRST LAWN HAD BEEN mowed haphazardly. Rusty first noticed it when leaving for work. It didn't look like it had been cut with a lawnmower or brush hog. Instead, someone had taken gardening shears to it, like someone had given the grass a haircut. Though it was a small lawn, it must have taken hours; the grass had been nearly three feet high. Most odd was the fact that there were no clippings lying in the street or in the yard. They had all been cleaned up, bagged, and taken elsewhere.

Rusty didn't think much of it and headed off to work. The next morning, though, another lawn had been sheared. The next day, another one. The next, two more. Whoever was cutting the lawns was getting more efficient, getting better. The grass no longer appeared uneven, hastily sliced up, blades resembling a haircut gone awry. Now the cuts seemed even and straight. Care had been taken. Meticulous precision. Pride.

The police responded soon thereafter. They canvassed the neighborhood, interviewing all of Rusty's neighbors to glean anything suspicious. A policewoman interviewed Rusty and Deborah. She had an odd appearance to her. Her face seemed inordinately asymmetrical. Rusty knew asymmetries to be present in all human bodies. His left arm, for instance, drooped about a half-inch longer than his right. But the policewoman's asymmetries were more pronounced—one eye was much larger than the other, and rounder, like it was a perfect circle; her right bicep was mannish, her left dainty; and she had an exquisite left butt cheek, plump and curvaceous, the other basically non-existent. Truth be told, she nearly looked deformed.

Deborah offered her tea, but she declined. "Caffeine makes me a little jumpy," she said. They convened in the living room. Rusty and Deborah sat on the sofa, their knees touching. Riley camped out in Rusty's recliner. It was too large for her, and her feet couldn't quite touch the ground.

"Tell me about Mr. Lindsey," the policewoman said. Her name was Rebecca, the only cop Rusty knew who introduced herself using her first name. "Has he seemed imbalanced lately? Troubled? Stressed?"

"You mean besides what happened the other morning?" Rusty asked.

She nodded.

"No." He looked to Deborah for assistance. "Nothing comes to mind."

"Has he been complaining about the city? About the law?"

"Everyone complains about it."

She nodded again, this time puckering her lips in frustration. Apparently she had received this same answer at his neighbors' houses.

"Have you seen anything suspicious? Heard anything the past three nights that sounded unusual?"

Rusty shook his head. "All quiet on the western front."

"I'm sorry?"

"No," he said. "Nothing at all."

"A Weed Eater or lawn mower or anything?"

"Nothing."

The policewoman sighed. The investigation was going nowhere; that much was obvious. Not that Rusty had expected it to go well. He and the neighbors had been talking. None of them had a clue as to who was cutting the lawns, for what purpose, and whose lawn would be next. It seemed isolated to their neighborhood—coworkers and friends living in other parts of the city reported no such mysterious cuttings. It was as if their small, middle-class neighborhood had a vigilante in its midst.

Rusty had to admit it was pretty exciting.

"Please," the policewoman said. "Give us a call if something arises. Anything at all. No matter how small."

FIRST, IT WAS A PAIR of rain boots. Then it was a jacket. Next was a wool beanie. Lost, Riley explained. She didn't have a clue as to where they ended up. Initially, Rusty didn't give it a second thought. She was a child after all, and weren't children prone to losing things? After that, Rusty found mud caked in her room, right underneath her window, dried into the fibers of the carpet. He found a tear in a sweater she hadn't worn in months, it being much too warm for such a garment. He found a ski mask tucked underneath her bed, a blade of grass sticking out of one of its eyeholes. Her fingers, he noticed, had calloused. She appeared tired. Purple bags floated underneath her eyes like half-moons. She slept in later on the weekends. Dirt lined her fingernails. Her skin had been stained red from clay.

"You don't think it's her, do you?" he asked Deborah as they sat in their bungalow's breakfast nook one Sunday morning, sipping coffee and eating day-old donut holes.

"No," she said. "Don't be ridiculous."

"But the sweater. The mud."

"She's probably sneaking out to go see friends. I used to do that. They're probably TP-ing someone. Or going to see a boy she has a crush on. She's not a criminal."

"Riley? Sneaking out to go see friends? A boy? *Our* daughter?"

Deborah sipped her coffee, popped her lips after she swallowed. "Our daughter is *not* a criminal."

"Okay. Okay. Then how do you explain what's going on?"

Deborah wiped her fingers on a dishtowel and then on her jeans. Her fingertips appeared to still be sticky, however, the donut glaze reflecting the sunlight shining through the bay window. Outside, Indian grass waved in the breeze like spectators at a football game. Before, Rusty had taken great pride in his lawn. It had been immaculate, so pristine he could've placed a putting green out there. Now, though, it resembled a forest, uninhabited by civilization. It was wild. It was native. It drove him nuts.

"Like I said," Deborah continued, "It's probably harmless. All kids sneak out of the house at some point. It's nothing to worry about."

He had half a mind to assist the vigilante; however, the private contractor had negotiated stiffer and stiffer penalties into the legislation for offences, going so far as a three-year prison sentence for mowing your own lawn. It would've made Rusty laugh if it wasn't so serious. Instead of fixing their initial debacle, the city council had made matters worse. The proof of it was living right next door to him. Gil, having made bail, was back at home after his incident, but he faced a trial in a few weeks determining his fate. Caught with a chainsaw, it seemed likely he would face jail time.

A minor had never been charged before. If his daughter was the vigilante, she could be taken away by the DHS, sent to a juvenile detention center. He wouldn't be able to see her for months, years even. It was unthinkable.

"We should talk to her."

"You're blowing this way out of proportion," Deborah said.

"Am I?" he asked. "Does she not maybe show anti-social behavior? You said so yourself."

Deborah slammed her open palm against the glass table. "Stop it!"

Startled, Rusty spilled some coffee in his lap. He yelped and jumped out of his seat and tried to wipe away the scalding liquid, but he could still feel it burning. He unbuckled his belt and shimmied his way out of his pants in an attempt to make the blistering pain go away. The flesh was pink and turning red, the skin somehow seeming thinner there than the surrounding areas. Just as his pants fell around his knees, Riley walked in. Without saying a word, she closed her eyes, then walked blindly out of the room.

SHE SNUCK OUT AT ABOUT 1:30 a.m. It was dark out, the moon covered by clouds, making it difficult to see. A ski mask covered her face, her hands were gloved, a backpack was flung over her shoulders. She seemed more like a spy than his daughter, which surprised Rusty. So careful, so inconspicuous. She'd always seemed more dazed to him, lost in her own little world. Not now, though. She had practiced this. She had done this before.

After a quick pause, she headed west down their street. She kept a slow and steady pace, stopping every dozen or so feet to take in her surroundings. Due to the overgrown lawns, he followed at a safe distance, careful not to let the crumple of the underbrush give away his position. At the end of the street, she turned north. She stayed low to the ground, darting next to a privacy fence. She continued on in this way for another block, then turned into an empty lot. Rusty hid about forty yards down the street behind some garbage cans. Only her head popped up above the weeds, a dark bulbous shadow absent of features. Waiting for her looked to be several more bulbous shadows, six by Rusty's count. The shadows appeared to be looking at Riley's new iPad—a luminous glow emanated from their center, and in a heated discussion, their heads bobbed, ponytails shaking feverishly.

He waited for a while. He counted to twenty, then seventy, then a hundred. Getting impatient, he almost blew his cover and walked over to the empty lot to tell his daughter to get her crap together and go on home. But then grass clippings sprayed into the air and fell back to the ground like confetti during a ticker-tape parade.

He was right! It *was* Riley cutting all those lawns. And she had accomplices.

Using shears and an antique push lawn mower, they mowed the empty lot in less than three hours. It was remarkable, really. They coordinated without much communication, each responsible for a particular piece of the lot. When they were finished, they planted a sign that simply read: "Brought to U by Anonymous."

Rusty didn't know what to do. He contemplated confronting her before they got back home, demanding some sort of explanation. He would do it, like a father should, feigning anger, although, if he was honest with himself, he was more afraid of the consequences if she got caught. He also considered telling Deborah, asking for her input before confronting Riley, but she would just deny the whole thing.

No. Best to confront her now.

He stayed behind the trash cans, not wanting to approach her in front of her accomplices. After they were finished, they convened out in front of their handiwork, and one reached into a backpack. He had tried to keep Riley in his sights during the night, but he had lost her soon after they began working. He was pretty sure this little girl was Riley as she pulled out what appeared to be the iPad he'd given to her for her birthday. She turned around, faced her work, and snapped a photograph. After some congratulatory hugs, the group dispersed, with Riley heading towards Rusty alone.

As soon as she reached him, he placed a hand on her shoulder. She jumped, dropping her backpack. When she looked up at Rusty, her eyes were like polished marble. She turned to run, but before she could get away, Rusty grabbed her arm.

The picture she had just taken already had more than 100 likes.

At home, he parked Riley in the living room. She had a defiant look on her face. Her feet dangled just above the carpet, mud caked around the soles of her shoes. She looked like she had when she was much younger, four or five maybe, when he had forced her to share with her cousins or made her stop sitting so close to the television. Basically, it was a look that said, "as soon as you turn your back, I'm going to do it again."

"What were you *thinking*?" Rusty asked. He knew he should be more delicate, understanding, but he was pissed. "And don't give me any of this 'I don't know' bull crap."

"I don't know."

"What did I just say?"

"I don't know. I don't know."

"You broke the law, Riley. Do you understand that?"

"Are you going to tell Mom?"

Riley wasn't worried what her father thought. He did not act as the disciplinarian in the house. Deborah did. He'd been relegated to a figurehead role, authoritarian in name only. This hurt more than he cared to admit.

"Mom is the least of your worries."

She crossed her arms and sank back into the chair.

"Seriously, Riley. You could go to jail. They'd lock you up, and you'd never be able to see us."

She rolled her eyes.

"Riley, please listen to me."

She hopped of her chair, her mud-soaked shoes squishing into the carpet. "I am, Daddy," she said as she kissed him on the forehead.


THE MOWING DIDN'T STOP. IF anything, it became more frequent. It had even spilled out of Rusty's immediate neighborhood. Some were a few miles away. Three or four or five would be cut per night, in different parts of the city, all of them signed "Anonymous." A movement had begun. Not all of these crimes could have been committed by these six preteen girls. That would've been impossible. They had sparked something, and it was not going away.

The nightly newscasts began to take notice. Investigative journalists searched for clues. The police asked for anyone who might have any tips to contact them immediately. Graffiti popped up, some in support of Anonymous, others opposed. The striking workers called them anti-union vigilantes, scabs and worse. Frustrated citizens called them harbingers of commonsense justice. People fought in the streets over it. The entire city seemed about to explode. Riots appeared to be imminent.

It didn't take the police long to locate the Facebook page. It took even less time to trace it back to Riley. They came when she was at school. It was the same policewoman as before, the one whose eye was three times the size of the other, constantly peering at him. Looking at her gave him vertigo.

"We thought we should let you know," she said, "police are on their way to pick up your daughter."

Rusty attempted to play dumb, but she wasn't buying it.

"As her parents, we wanted to give you the opportunity to be there when we did."

They drove to the school, a few miles away. As they did, Rusty couldn't help but notice that the neighborhood looked like it had before, not all that long ago, pristine and immaculate. Dew glistened off mowed grass. Bushes were trimmed into perfect, straight lines. He had to admit; those kids did one hell of a fine job.

At the school, six police cars idled out in the bus loop. A crowd had already gathered, wondering what the commotion was. Concerned parents pointed at the school, their heads bobbing as they chastised the administration for not letting them know what was going on; it was, after all, *their* kids inside.

Rebecca and Rusty made their way through the crowd to get into the school, but they were stopped by a uniformed police officer.

"We have the school shut down, sir," the policeman said as he placed a hand on Rusty's chest. The policeman tried to glare at him, but the look was almost comical as the policeman was severely cross-eyed.

"This is the father," Rebecca said, jabbing her thumb into Rusty's chest. It hurt, the nail digging into the flesh just above his nipple, and he had to rub it to dull the ache.

"The kid's missing."

"What?" Rusty asked. "Missing?"

"We got the whole area on lockdown searching for her."

"What do you mean, 'missing'?"

"She shouldn't get far," he continued. "With all the lawns mowed, she has fewer places to hide."

Not knowing what to do, Rusty started to run. He had no idea where to run to, though. Her favorite place in the world was in her bedroom, curled up with a book. But she wouldn't go there; she was too smart for that. As far as Rusty was aware, she had no other place of refuge, no sanctuary to be alone, to reflect, or hide in. All of a sudden, Rusty felt sorry for his daughter. No one, especially a child, should be deprived of that.

Rebecca chased behind him, calling for him to stop. Because he had no idea where he was going, he obliged. Winded, he bent over, gasping to catch his breath.

"We'll find her," she said. "Don't worry. We will find her."

THE SEARCH PARTY WAS LARGE. There were dozens of police, neighbors, kids from the school, firefighters, paramedics, gym teachers, even bureaucrats from the DMV. They all started at the school, building a perimeter, and then proceeded outward, calling out "Riiiiileeeeeeey!" every few steps. Deborah stood with Rusty, hand in hand, on the north side of the building and headed away from their home.

Deborah still wouldn't believe her little girl could be responsible for all of this. School fields were mowed. Houses free of trash and dirt. Gutters reattached to roofs. The city began to look like a city again, a place of civilization, and Deborah couldn't have been more embarrassed. Her daughter, a criminal. Rusty had to admit that he, too, felt ashamed. He'd thought he taught his little girl better than this.

"Riley!" he called out.

Nothing—just the whine of a tired and old dog off in the distance.

Then came a buzz in his pocket, his cell phone. He ignored it at first, but then it came again. His phone would continue to buzz until he acknowledged the message, so he pulled out his phone. It was a Facebook message from Riley.

It said: "I can hear your voice."

He typed back, "Where are you?"

"What are you doing?" Deborah asked.

He shook his head.

"Seriously, our daughter is in trouble and,—" She looked over his shoulder. "—and you're checking your Facebook page? What the hell is wrong with you?"

A message returned from Riley: "I'm under the Rocket Ship Bridge."

The Rocket Ship Bridge was in Stephenson Park just around the corner. Rusty whispered into his wife's ear, "I know where she is. Cover for me." She had a reticent look on her face, but she nodded. When he turned to slip away, her fingertips pressed against his with just a little more pressure than usual. Go get our daughter, the gesture said. She's the most important thing right now.

Rusty slipped away and headed over to Stephenson Park. Calls for his daughter echoed over the treetops. They were close and getting closer. It wouldn't take long for at least one of the search parties to find her. It was just a matter of time.

The Rocket Ship Bridge sat between two large play rocket ships. They had stairs and slides for children to play and have fun. Riley was curled up underneath the bridge, sitting with her iPad in her lap. She perused pictures of all that she had done and inspired across the city. Lawns were mowed. People were posing and smiling in front of their homes once again. Someone had tagged "Anonymous" on an overpass. There was a video for that one. Each time a car passed underneath, the driver honked his horn in support. It was difficult not to feel pride, even if Riley was a criminal. She had done what he and Deborah had asked—she had reached out and connected with the world. She had effected change in others, and Riley would never be the same. She would, after now, no longer be anonymous.

"Everyone's looking for you, sweetie," Rusty said.

"I know," Riley said.

"Is that why you ran?"

She nodded.

"Are you scared?"

She nodded.

Rusty scooted in next to her and put his arm around her shoulder, comforting her. Despite the circumstances, he enjoyed this little moment. To be needed was every father's wish.

Riley placed her head on his shoulder. "I just wanted to help Mr. Lindsey out," she said. "That was all. He just seemed so upset about everything that I thought if I could help him out, he'd be happier."

"That was very thoughtful of you."

"I guess I just took it a little too far."

"It happens. I understand."

"What's going to happen to me?"

She peered up at her father. Her eyes were buoyant and moist. Her fear broke Rusty's heart. He just wanted to hold her and protect her forever.

He helped her up to her feet. "Follow me," he said. "Everything is going to be okay."

They came out from underneath the bridge. There, standing in the street, was the search party Rusty had just left.

"You will have to go with that lady there," he said, pointing to Rebecca.

"But why, Daddy?" she asked. "Why?"

"You broke the rules, Riley. When you break the rules, you have to be punished."

Riley began to sob. It wasn't a loud wail, but a slow and steady cry. She wiped her eyes with her sleeve. Deborah tried to go to Riley, but the asymmetrical policewoman held her back, then headed toward Rusty and Riley. Before she could take Riley away, however, Rusty leaned in to whisper in her ear.

"The city looks good, sweetie," he said. "You did good."

Riley smiled and nodded, sniffling back the last of her tears. "See you soon, Dad."

"Real soon," he said.

Rusty took Riley's hand and then passed her over to Rebecca, who radioed in that the fugitive was in custody, officially ending the search.

Rebecca placed Riley in the backseat of a nearby police cruiser and then shut the door. Riley looked out the window, her face long and confused. The search party bore witness. All of them were silent. It reminded Rusty of a vigil, as if they had congregated for a collective mourning, to heal and to move forward, and to make peace with what they had done.

# Amid the Flood of Mortal Ills

AT FIRST THEY DIDN'T KNOW WHAT TO THINK—THEY'D HEARD ALL ALONG THAT IT WAS POSSIBLE, THE oceans rising so that a majority of the US would be under water—but as the *what if* turned into reality and Florida and then Mississippi and then Louisiana and then Massachusetts all became submerged, those in the Midwest couldn't all help but realize, almost instantaneously, like a shared dream across thousands of miles, that everything would be different from then on. Their cushy, easy, selfish lives no longer existed.

Benji worked on the Skyline Luxury Condominiums as a welder. His office was a steel beam a foot wide and twenty stories up and provided a remarkable view. A little ways out into the harbor Benji saw a large yacht with smoke rising from the deck. The passengers appeared to be barbecuing. Benji couldn't help but be jealous. He hadn't had a steak in months. He tried not to let it bother him, though. He had too many other worries. With all the refugees and the shortage of land, his rent had quadrupled for his small apartment, costing him nearly $4,000 a month for a basement studio; food prices had skyrocketed—an ear of corn was about $10—and he had a kid on the way. A wife and baby to feed and put a roof over. He was going to be a father. *Him*. He could hardly believe it.

He returned to the job at hand, welding a steel beam to an L-joint supporting what would be the twenty-first floor. It was a cool job, he had to admit; he enjoyed the welding and he even enjoyed the height. But he was afraid the levees wouldn't hold and he would go tumbling end over end into an unfathomably deep and unforgiving ocean.

Looking back out to the barbecue he noticed panic aboard the yacht. Flames licked the sky from the deck, much larger than they should've been. The fire had leapt from the grill and set the boat on fire. Several people scrambled, shooting the fire with extinguishers, but the blaze quickly spread and became stronger. That was when he realized that no one was going to help. The Coast Guard wasn't scrambling to their rescue. He could do nothing. Not from here. And neither could his coworkers. Each of them stopped working one by one, and stared out at the flames as the passengers dove into the crystal blue waters. They didn't have any other choice. It was either stay put and burn to death or jump and swim to safety. Then the yacht sank.

SUMMER, BENJI'S WIFE, GREETED HIM with a hug and a kiss on the cheek and a "How was your day, honey?" when he got home that evening.

"Good," he said. And it was. "Saw a boat sink."

"Really?" He nodded. "Oh my God! Was anyone hurt?"

He shrugged. "I don't think so. They weren't too far out. I saw three or four make it to land."

"Jesus. I hope they're all okay," she said, more to herself than to Benji.

He kissed her belly, and he could feel the baby squirm. Summer flinched. At seven months, she'd been experiencing a lot of pain. The doctor had said that was all normal, though, and they shouldn't worry. Their baby was healthy and would be beautiful. Summer said she just wanted the damn thing out of her.

Their little basement apartment didn't have any windows, so despite it still being daylight outside, their living room looked like it was past midnight. One lamp cast the room in an orange glow, and dust swam through the air like a school of jellyfish. It became hard to breathe at times. The floor was being eaten away by water damage so that the cracked concrete foundation showed. They were sick all the time because of it, both of them suffering from chronic coughs and walking pneumonia. Benji had promised himself and Summer that before their child was born he would find them a better place to live. But there just wasn't anything out there. Scanning the classifieds didn't help; the rooms were gone before the ink had dried on the paper. More people migrated every day, and unless you were lucky enough to be in the right place at the right time, literally at the landlord's doorstep when the house or apartment or condo became available, you didn't have a chance at landing it. That was just their new reality.

"News said the water rose twenty feet today," Summer said. "Twice as much as they were expecting."

"Any cause yet?"

"They're clueless. I don't even think they're trying to figure it out anymore."

She set the table. Instant potatoes and hot dogs. Fresh produce and meat were impossible to come by. Too little food for too many mouths. Why they were bringing in another was beyond Benji. He and Summer had planned the pregnancy. They'd talked about it. How great it would be to have a baby around the house. The little pitter-patter of footsteps. They never discussed the burdens a baby would bring. The sacrifices. The kind of world they were going to be bringing him or her up in. Their decision was shortsighted and naïve, maybe, but it was something to look forward to.

"Do you think the levees will hold?" Summer asked.

"Hard to tell."

She paused a moment, cradling her belly with her arms like a basket of bread. "What'll we do if they don't?"

They avoided this subject, too, like if they discussed it, it would imminently happen. By doing so, they were able to cling to the belief that the waters would cease to rise, recede even, and uncover more land so that the refugees could start anew, so that they could, too. It was a childish impulse, to ignore their problems in hopes that they would go away of their own volition. But they weren't the only ones that did this; Benji was sure of it. Perhaps all of humanity suffered from a chronic plague of arrested development.

On the news the government offered suggestions, to stay calm, to get on the roof of your house, to stay put until someone came to rescue you. No one Benji knew planned on taking that advice.

Summer flinched, grabbed her stomach and sat down. Benji jumped to her, afraid she was going into labor prematurely. She grimaced, her eyes watered, and the veins in her face looked like they could pop at any moment. He stood by her, waiting for her to give him instructions on what he should do. He knew better than to talk. Summer breathed quick, irregular breaths. She grabbed his arm and dug her nails into his skin. This was the worst it had ever been. Benji was convinced she was going into labor, that he needed to grab her and carry her upstairs and try to catch a bus so that they could get to the hospital to have their baby, their baby, dear God, they were having a baby.

For the first time, the fact that Summer and he were having a baby *really* sank in. It was like he could feel the entire weight of the universe bearing down on him. The burden was so immense, so strangling, so paralyzing that he stopped breathing, and he was overcome with this sudden overwhelming urge to flee and to never come back.

Eventually, though, Summer's shoulders relaxed, her breathing returned to normal, and her nails no longer dug into his flesh. For a few moments they sat there in silence, Benji's arms wrapped around Summer's shoulders, and her chin resting on his arm.

"We're not stupid, are we?" Summer asked.

"I don't know," Benji said. "Could be."

THEY WENT SHOPPING THE NEXT day, Benji's day off, for baby stuff. They couldn't afford much, so they milled around second-hand stores. They purchased a teddy bear and a stroller and different books they had read when they were kids: *Winnie the Pooh* and *Curious George* and *Prince Caspian*. The stroller was missing a wheel, but Benji could fashion one out of something, perhaps steal a wheelbarrow wheel from work. They bought used blankets and pillows and one of those toys that attaches to the crib and plays lullabies. Nothing fancy, but Benji was glad to be able do this one domestic thing, as if life still resembled some sort of normalcy.

As they left the store, their new belongings crammed high in a wobbly shopping cart, the sirens sounded. Summer and Benji were in the parking lot, halfway to the bus stop when they heard them. Back before the flood, they had been used as tornado sirens, but now they denoted one thing: a levee might break. The parking lot was mostly deserted. They didn't have to worry about panicked crowds or mobs of people. But they didn't know what to do, either. They'd both seen images of what had happened. The water destroyed everything. Buildings were demolished, cars tossed, trees uprooted, bridges collapsed. And there wasn't any stopping it. Oklahoma was flat ground. If the levees failed, they all would die.

So, with no other option at hand, Summer and Benji peered around them, waiting for the water to submerge the city where they had both grown up and lived their entire lives. They didn't cry or hold hands or say that they loved each other. They didn't see the point. They just waited for their oncoming destruction.

But the waters never came. Eventually the sirens ceased, and they could hear the birds and cars and trains again. It was a false alarm. They'd had more and more of those lately, once every few weeks it seemed. They hardly fazed Benji and Summer anymore, really. The bus even came on time, full to the hilt of other people, dazed like them, staring blankly out the windows.

ONE OF THE FEW LUXURIES Summer and Benji maintained was a family doctor, Dr. Foley. They had an ultrasound appointment, and they hurried after dropping off their new items at their apartment and ended up only being fifteen minutes late, a new record.

Dr. Foley's office was located in an old daycare that had shut down because of problems with the Department of Human Services. This had happened before the flood, actually. Benji remembered having read about it, something about one of the women running the place inappropriately touching a few of the toddlers. Forced oral sodomy or something like that.

The nurse called Summer's name, and she and Benji were led toward the back. Summer weighed in, and then they went back to the examination room where the nurse took Summer's blood pressure. It was elevated, 140/90, and the nurse pursed her lips and made a sucking noise, almost as if she'd expected this, and told Summer that the doctor would be in to see her shortly.

Doctor's offices had always given Benji the creeps. Despite doctors' attempts to make examination rooms welcoming and warm, they always seemed so cold. The examination tables, the hand sanitizer, the biohazard waste bins, all of it covered in protective paper, plastic, and latex, smelling of disinfectant and chemicals. He was always afraid he was going to catch something when he visited, a cold, the flu, something even worse like Ebola, where his organs would melt and seep from the inside out.

Dr. Foley came in. She looked tired and weary, like she hadn't slept in days, eyes bruise-purple and swollen. "How're things?" she asked with a more upbeat tone than he'd heard in a while. Her bedside manner was probably second nature. "Good, I hope."

"About as well as they can be," Summer said. "We haven't drowned yet."

Dr. Foley forced a chuckle and snapped on some latex gloves. She smiled, prepared her stethoscope, and listened to Summer's heartbeat. "I'm worried about your blood pressure," she said. "It's awfully high."

"Considering the circumstances…" Summer trailed off.

"No excuse," Dr. Foley said. "Have you noticed anything irregular?"

"Irregular?"

"Discolored urine. Lower back pain."

"I'm pregnant. What do you think?"

"Have you been drinking enough fluids? Getting enough rest?"

"Does anybody?"

The doctor grabbed an otoscope and examined Summer's ears. Summer rubbed her hands together like she had terrible arthritis.

"Eating healthy? Morning sickness?" Dr. Foley asked.

"Option one no. Option two absolutely. Feel like I spend half my time in front of the toilet."

"I get the feeling you aren't taking this seriously."

"Just tell us what's wrong!" Benji yelled.

Both the doctor and Summer blinked at him and leaned back as if they needed to get a better view.

"Nothing is wrong," Dr. Foley said. "Yet. If Summer's high blood pressure continues, it could damage her kidneys and the baby could be born prematurely."

"Might?"

"It's just a possibility."

Summer placed her hand atop Benji's and patted to reassure him. "That's it?"

"Well," Dr. Foley said, "there's a remote possibility that you could develop preeclampsia."

"Oh, preeclampsia. Of course. Why didn't I think of that?" Benji said.

"And what does that mean?" Summer asked.

"It could lead to seizures. Stillbirth. The mother's death."

"The mother's death?" Summer asked.

"Your death." The doctor readied the ultrasound machine and then plopped neon blue gel onto Summer's stomach. "But like I said, it's a very remote possibility. Odds are you're going to be fine. Just fine."

A picture appeared on the monitor. It was one of those three-dimensional images where Benji and Summer could make out the baby's features. This was the first time they'd been able to see their baby in such high definition. Benji could make out the little nose and ears and fingers and its clamped-shut eyes, and he couldn't help but stare in disbelief. This tiny little thing would forever be in their care. There was no escaping that fact. It would come. It was inevitable. The sun would rise, flowers would bloom, taxes would be due, rent would have to be paid, the waters would rise, it would be born and Benji couldn't help but think this was wrong. All of it. Summer and him and the baby—every last bit of it.

It was a boy. A baby boy. Benji never really had a preference, boy or girl. It didn't really matter to him as long as he or she was healthy. He had to admit, though, his preference for health didn't stem out of any concern for the child itself. The baby had always been more of an idea, an abstraction. Mainly, his concern was that he wouldn't be able to afford a sick child. But now, once he had seen the baby during the 3D ultrasound, his child had become real. The baby was now tangible, and the burden he carried palpable.

BENJI GOT TO WORK BEFORE dawn. Floodlights illuminated the skeletal structure of the high-rise. Red steel loomed up above, and a light mist fell, making the scene look almost eerie. He clocked in and lumbered into the elevator car along with his co-workers, but before they felt the familiar jolt of the elevator moving up, his boss ambled out of the darkness. He looked tired and dirty, as if he'd been working for hours already.

"The levee," he said, gasping for breath, "we need every man at the levee."

Before he had time to explain, he dragged Benji and the others to his truck. They drove through the deserted streets the five miles to the levee. It was too early for most to be about, readying for their days at work, sneaking in a cup of coffee and whatever food they could scrounge up. Benji was thankful for that. At least they had a few more moments of peace before they awoke to the levees being breached. Just like with the high-rise, floodlights illuminated the concrete. The wall sparkled with mist and Benji could smell the salt even more strongly than usual. His boss led them to an impromptu elevator powered by pulleys and levers rather than a generator. Benji'd worked enough construction to know that this was an emergency. As they lurched upward, a dread came over him and settled into the pit of his stomach like acid.

The view over the levee stunned Benji. The waters had travelled inland nearly a mile and the surface sat only a few feet below the top of the levee. Perhaps the siren he'd heard yesterday hadn't been a false alarm but a genuine scare. Hundreds of men scrambled in the dark, applying mortar and building the wall even higher. They worked tirelessly, shoveling and lifting, cranes swinging steel beams as quickly as they could. An operation of this magnitude would take weeks, even months of planning in advance, but yet this had come to fruition almost overnight. It was such an awesome sight, really, that Benji couldn't help but be astounded.

Boats travelled the length of the wall carrying supplies. It was odd the waters were so calm. Benji expected to see large waves crashing, knocking workmen over, and whitecaps as tall as buildings. But, instead, the waters looked like a vast, opaque mirror, reflecting the night sky in a deep navy.

"It won't hold for long," Benji's boss said. He was a big man, had been working construction longer than Benji had been alive, and had canine-like jowls and bicuspids. "We got to raise this wall along a half-mile by tonight if we're going to survive until tomorrow." He slapped Benji on the back. "Get to work."

Benji could feel the humidity and the salt in the air. Sweat and sea clung to his pores so that his flesh took on the texture of sandpaper. A man, his face cast in shadow, handed Benji a wheelbarrow full of brick. Looking at this familiar tool, he couldn't help but think that the wheel would fit his unborn son's stroller perfectly.

The man pointed down the line. In the dark Benji couldn't make out where exactly the man was pointing, but he headed in that direction anyway. The walkway was narrow, and men smoothed grout in order to fix more brick to the wall. They cemented each one by hand. Small bricks. Stone. Marble. Granite. Limestone. There was no plan. No engineers or architects. These were just random men, building random segments out of random materials. The wall wouldn't hold. Benji knew it wouldn't. Later this morning the waters would break through the dam and destroy the city. Worse yet, there wasn't any place to run. If the waters had risen like this here, it would be the same worldwide. The whole Earth would soon be under water.

Benji's immediate thought was to call Summer. But what would he tell her? That the end was near and he wouldn't be able to make it home in time? That she would spend the last moments on Earth alone and so would he? He couldn't do that to her. It'd be better if she was asleep. Maybe the city wouldn't even sound the sirens. What would be the point? There would just be panic. Let them go peacefully. It was the least they could do.

The sea began to churn. Tumultuous waves crashed into the wall, sending the waters up and over the men. Some even fell the few stories to the ground. The boats carrying supplies rocked back and forth, the men fighting to hold on and not fall overboard. Bricks dropped. Benji heard screams. They didn't seem to come from anyone in particular. They were just random. Some close. Others far away. But all were frightened.

A man reached for Benji. He was in a canoe. The supplies he had been carrying were already unloaded or overboard. He pleaded with Benji to help him, to pull him to safety. Benji grabbed his arm and tugged until he had two feet firmly on the wall. "Thank you," he said. "You saved my life."

The oars were still in their holsters as the canoe bobbed and thrashed. Benji expected the small boat to be taken away, smashed into pieces against the levee. But it stayed put as if tethered there, though Benji could see that it was not.

As all the other men clamored down the wall, the waters calmed as suddenly as they had turned violent, the whitecaps returned to the dark blue of the sea, and the waves ceased to chop. The waters had risen several feet in a matter of seconds. And there was the canoe still, floating next to the wall, the city's last, great hope at survival.

The sirens began to blare as the sun broke the horizon and the first rays of morning light illuminated the city. Benji's eardrums throbbed from the sirens, and he knew that once the sea overflowed he would die. His wife would die. His unborn son would die. Everyone he knew or did know or would ever have known would soon be dead. His cushy, selfish life would be lost amid the flood of mortal ills.

But if he stepped out onto the canoe and paddled away, he could stall the inevitable. He would still die, but he would not die from the flood. From exposure maybe. Or hunger. But not by the waters. To be the last human being alive. What would that *feel* like?

He stepped out into the canoe and faced the city. Hundreds of people stared back at him, frozen in terror in the streets. None seemed content with their fate. But none fought it either. They simply stood idly by, waiting for the end to come. Benji grabbed the oars, but before he pushed off and rowed out to sea, he waved to them. Not one of them waved back.

Those poor people, he thought. If only they could help themselves.

# Disobedience

ALAN HAD JUST LOADED HIS TRUNK AND WAS RETURNING HIS CART TO THE BIN WHEN HE WAS STOPPED for a few seconds, that was all, cornered by Mrs. Fourkiller. She asked about the impending school district consolidation, and he asked how Scrappy, her husband, was doing, if he'd gained mobility in his knee since the car accident, and then when he turned around, a mother to one of his students, Amber Montgomery, was screaming.

The IGA parking lot wasn't packed by any means. A high-school boy herded up shopping carts—Brentley was his name—a long train stretched out in front of him. Mary Redtree, a first-year history teacher, packed the trunk of her hatchback with brown paper bags. A Honda Civic parked in a handicap spot. Parents dragged their children behind them. A few old men, their cowboy hats prim and spotless, chewed tobacco on the bench by the newspaper rack. It was a typical Saturday afternoon, trash blowing around in the harsh spring breeze.

"*Amber!*" her mother yelled, hands cupped around her mouth. She let go of her shopping cart, and it rolled down the inclined parking lot, crashing finally into an old minivan. "Amber!" she yelled. "Please! Answer me!"

He'd watched Amber while in the store, followed her down the dog food aisle and past the frozen food section and the deli meats, contemplating whether or not he should speak. She was seventeen and pretty in a diffident sort of way. She wasn't popular or well regarded by her teachers, and when Alan would run across her in school, she was often alone in the library, perusing how-to books for surviving in the wilderness or large-game hunting. She rarely smiled, and when she did, she covered her mouth with her hand. He'd always made an effort to speak with her when he saw her, to say hello and ask her how her studies were going, life at home. At first, she was shy when he asked, but after a while she warmed up to him, and about once per week she would stop by his office to ask his advice about one thing or another, if she should take the ACT or maybe just get a job after graduation in Bartlesville or Tulsa. Alan had to admit that he enjoyed these little meetings—they were the only times he ever felt he made a difference in his position—but lately teachers and parents and students had started to spread rumors of an inappropriate relationship. He'd been thinking he should speak with Amber about this when she spotted him watching her. They'd been in the produce section near the exit, and she approached him with her arms clasped in front of her like she had to protect herself, and Alan couldn't help but be a little hurt by this—he didn't, after all, wish her any harm.

Out in the parking lot, her mother ran the aisles. She called out Amber's name and ran around the back of the store. She looked under cars. She looked in the alcove where the unused shopping carts were stored. She even looked in the big blue dumpster. She looked and looked and looked, and Alan just stood there watching her—they all did: Brentley and Mrs. Fourkiller and the old men— none of them offering to help.


THE SCHOOL HAD NO MONEY. That was just the plain reality, and no matter what Alan did, that wouldn't change. The sooner the staff understood that fact, the quicker they could move on, plan for the inevitable—them losing their jobs, their students being absorbed into larger school districts, Bartlesville mostly, their dying town mercifully relieved of its last, wheezing gasp. Evidence of the situation surrounded all of them. He didn't even have a door on his office anymore, just a curtain. An unruly student had shattered the glass, and instead of replacing it he just took it off its hinges. It now resided in the basement, stored away in the corner of the school's tornado shelter.

But here was Ms. Redtree, asking for money. "The Land Run is a part of this state's identity," she explained. "The kids deserve to know what happened."

"I'm not saying don't teach them. They have books. Use those. A re-creation of the event is entirely unnecessary. And not within our budget."

"Please don't be condescending. I am well aware they have textbooks. Outdated, but they have them."

Alan sighed and pinched his nose like he was holding in a

sneeze. "I'm not trying to be condescending. I'm trying to tell you the truth."

"These kids deserve this," she said. "They need to get out of the classroom. They need learning to be fun. They need to get their minds off their missing classmate."

*Fun?* Was she serious?

This was why he never should've hired a rookie teacher. They graduated from college full of hope and idealism and principle. They had fantasies of being Robin Williams in *Dead Poet's Society*, students addressing an abusive authority figure and proclaiming their love for their dutiful teacher, "O Captain! My Captain!" Alan was sure he'd been that authority figure in many of Ms. Redtree's daydreams. She had that look about her, wistful. Her hair flittered about her face, and the whites of her eyes were bright, not like his, yellowed and reddened by years of no sleep and a three-drink minimum in his recliner.

"What if I paid for the supplies myself?" Ms. Redtree asked.

"Yourself? On *your* salary?"

"Now you're being condescending and offensive."

He wished he could have a taste of Scotch right then. He'd never brought a bottle to school, unlike some of the teachers, Mr. Appleberry for sure. The school guidance counselor, he smelled of peppermint schnapps every day by lunch, so Alan was sure not to send any impressionable students his way past eleven. He would be apt to give the kid a pull. Perhaps he could visit him after this meeting. It's not like he'd get fired. The district would only be open a few more weeks. Why hire an interim principal? Not even the

Department of Education was that dense.

"All I'm saying is that maybe you should be concentrating on saving your money rather than wasting it on this project."

"Some of us, Mr. Donahue, did not get into teaching for its fiduciary rewards."

That was right; he *wouldn't* get fired. Not yet anyway. So why did he care what he spent the district's money on? Who needed a prom? Most of the kids didn't go, and the seniors' banquet was more of a grim reminder of who didn't graduate than a celebration of those who did. Besides, if he could just get her to shut up about it, it would make the last remaining weeks of the semester that much easier to deal with.

"Fine," he said. "Whatever. I'll find the cash."

"You won't regret this, Mr. Donahue. Thank you."

Ms. Redtree stood and hurried out of his office before he could change his mind. He turned in his chair and stared out the window at the tattered yard. Years before it had been the football field, but the bleachers had long ago been torn down, the scraps probably dragged to homes for firewood. Now the yard was coarse with limestone gravel and spotted with cracked red clay. That's where they would end up having the Land Run. He could see it then, all sixty-seven of his students lined up with Radio Flyers with sheets draped over them, their covered wagons, waiting for some damn fool to blow a whistle so they could mark out territory that had once been promised to the displaced tribes—their ancestors. It'd be sad if the irony wouldn't be lost on all those kids.

ALAN LIVED JUST OUTSIDE OF Pawhuska where a tree line backed up into some rolling hills. The woods were intertwined with post oaks and blackjack and Indian grass. Limestone bedded streams, tributaries to Bluestem Lake, and murky water trickled through creeks where very little, if anything, swam. Whitetails pranced in gullies and squirrels skittered through the underbrush and avocets nested in branches. Every once in a while, a rifle shot would echo over the treetops. At night, coyotes howled at the moon like scavengers. It was a place Alan loved—he hunted big game, deer and mountain lion, the occasional wild boar. He would fish big-mouth at the lake and camp with friends so that he could drink beer without the PTA finding out. For the past thirty years there hadn't been a week gone by that he hadn't spent some time out there. It was a land he knew well. He knew the smell of the dirt. He knew every tree by name. He knew its story. In 1835, the federal government had guaranteed it to the Cherokee by the Treaty of New Echota. It didn't matter the Osage already called the land home. Wars broke out constantly. Not in the grand terms learned in history books. There weren't large massacres or battles fought by legions of warriors in open fields. Hundreds didn't die in hand-to-hand combat. Instead, cattle and horses were stolen. Men were murdered one or two at a time. Crops destroyed. Subterfuge and mayhem.

Remnants of those times trickled down to today. Legends mostly. Since Amber's disappearance, the one most prevalent in Alan's mind was about the Little People. Before the wars, stories had abounded. Short, squatty men who could fly and played pranks on villagers, they hid personal belongings, a prized beaded necklace, or new moccasins, giggling and stamping around a hunter alone in the woods. After the Cherokee relocation, the stories turned malevolent. Warlords and chiefs learned they could use the legend as psychological warfare. They perpetuated threats that the Little People would steal the young of those who committed crimes against other tribes. During the night, scouts would kidnap the children of rival communities, and a day or two later they would find their young hanged from a redbud tree.

The largest mass kidnapping in American history took place on Alan's land. More than fifty children were taken and later found not a few miles into the woods, dismembered into several pieces, arms and legs and heads. That was in 1839. A few years back, Alan had found a little shrine where the bodies had been found. He had no idea who'd built it. It wasn't much: a group of large stones piled atop one another, blocks of slate that reached about twenty feet high. Every few weeks or so he'd go out there and just sit. It was peaceful out there. He wouldn't be troubled by worldly things, his students' failing test scores, their rising dropout rate, the state's threat to shut down the school. He would simply sit in a lawn chair and listen to the sounds of the woods, sometimes dozing off. In those few moments between sleep and waking, he would think he could hear the pitter-patter of footsteps, the Little People coming in close to pull one of their pranks. It had to be them. Everything was just too goddamn funny.

THE TEACHERS WEREN'T EVEN SHOWING up to school anymore. Substitutes came in, his students' grandparents, who'd seen every last rerun *M\*A\*S\*H* had to offer and were thrilled to have an excuse to get out of the nursing home. Between classes, he would share a little snort with a few of them as he passed them in the hallway. Why the hell not? They needed a little excitement in their lives. One of the few who still showed, though, was Ms. Redtree. The district had already started shipping out desks and chalkboards and projectors, storing them for use in the Bartlesville Alternative Academy come next fall, so Ms. Redtree was having class outside each day, lecturing about the Trail of Tears as the children were gnawed raw by mosquitoes. Alan and Blinky, an old geezer who volunteered to watch gym class from nine to eleven each morning, would sip from paper cups and look on like spectators who couldn't afford a ticket. Freeloaders most would call them.

Ms. Redtree had rolled out an old whiteboard into the courtyard where the students would gather and smoke Pall Malls between classes. She diagrammed the southern United States, showing where and how far the Cherokee and other southern tribes had to walk back in the 1830s, driven by gunpoint from their homes. She would write fractions on the board, most notably 4,000/15,000. Four thousand had died on the trail. They were buried along riverbanks and at tree lines without stone or façade to mark them. Some were cast out into rivers, rocks tied to their arms and legs so they would sink. Others were simply left by the trail, the soldiers too busy to stop and dispose of the body. Yet these were simple, stale facts to the students, not the tragic history of their ancestors' fate. They would need to regurgitate it on a state exam at the end of the school year, but then they were free to forget it and focus on the importance of how to throw rocks at the Santa Fe railroad cars that ambled past, at least during good times when the oil rigs still chugged along. If not, they were forced to pick up cans along the road and take them to the recycling plant in Bartlesville so that they could collect change for food money. Regardless, they had more important things to do than learn from their teacher.

To mark the end of period, Susan, a lithe girl with cheekbones like cue balls, stood and bounced on her legs like a gymnast unfolding out of a cartwheel.

"Criminal," Blinky said. "Only time I ever get an erection is when I stare at underage girls."

"Jesus, Blinky. You can't tell me those sorts of things."

The old man snorted. "I'm just saying. It's nice to feel something down there every once in a while. Most of the time I'm afraid the twig is dead." He took a drink from his cup, the wine staining his lips merlot purple. "Tell me," he said. "You ever get with that Amber girl? The one that's missing."

"Where'd you hear that?" Alan asked.

"I wouldn't blame you if you did," Blinky continued. "Honestly, I don't see how you restrain yourself sometimes with all this young tail walking around here."

"Seriously, Blinky. Where'd you hear that?"

Blinky shrugged. "Around," he said. "People talk. Half the time it's bullshit."

"And the other half?"

He shrugged again. "Just watered-down bullshit."

The class dispersed. Ms. Redtree tried to corral them back into the school, but most of them, the boys anyway, scattered to the parking lot where they would climb into their trucks and find a secluded place to smoke some pot. Used to, Alan would try to stop this. Now he didn't see the point. He even had half a mind to join them.

"Another day in the books," Blinky said. "See you tomorrow." He patted Alan on the shoulder before parting, almost a consoling gesture. *Yes*, it seemed to say, *there will be a tomorrow. I'm truly sorry for that.*

Alan wandered into the school to gather his things so he could head home and try to find the strength to heat up a frozen chicken-fried steak instead of having a dinner, for the third night in a row, that consisted of sunflower seeds and Scotch. The halls were thin with students. Since he'd been teaching, the dropout rate had climbed exponentially. For every student who graduated, four dropped out. They weren't bad kids by any means. Most ended up needing to work in order to support their families, who, for whatever reason, didn't qualify for welfare benefits or had been swindled out of their social security or had become disabled from mesothelioma poisoning from the old tire factory out on Highway 80. The kids wound up working for the county underage, laying asphalt and welding old bridges. It was illegal to hire anyone under eighteen, but no one complained. There wasn't much of a workforce around here anymore. If the kids couldn't do it, it wouldn't get done.

As Alan gathered his papers—his résumé and last Sunday's crossword—someone knocked on the wall outside his office. It was Sheriff Whetsel, looking, it seemed, for a place to spit tobacco juice. He was a surly man now, gruff and with a short temper. Alan remembered him as Jeff, though, a cranky kid who'd whined every time an essay was assigned.

"What can I do for you, Sheriff?" Alan asked.

Jeff motioned with his hand as though he was drinking an imaginary glass of water. Alan grabbed an empty water bottle from his desk and handed it to the sheriff, who unscrewed the cap and spit into it. Black liquid slid down the edge of the bottle, tiny remnants of tobacco sticking to the clear plastic.

"Had a few questions for you, Mr. Donahue," he said, "about the missing girl."

Alan motioned for the sheriff to take a seat, and he did, slouching the way teenagers would when in trouble.

"Not sure how much I can help," Alan said. "She didn't have any enemies that I know of. Wasn't bullied. Had her problems at home like any other kid her age, but I never thought she'd run away."

"Eyewitnesses put you at the scene when she disappeared," the sheriff said. "Some say they even saw you with her, but you didn't stick around to give a statement."

Alan shook his head.

"Seems odd for a prominent member of the community, the high school principal, to leave the scene of the crime, don't you think? Especially since you knew the girl."

"To be fair," Alan said, "I didn't know she was missing at the time. Or that it was a crime scene."

"Did you see her while in the store?"

"Yes," Alan said.

"Did you speak with her?"

"Yes."

"And what did you two talk about?"

Lies. The lies they should tell. The importance of keeping their mouths shut. Anything but the truth, that it had happened after school when Amber came by the office to talk about her trouble with her mother, how she'd been drinking too much and how she was dating some guy who worked for Phillips 66 over in Bartlesville and who Amber thought might be a pervert. He'd just learned that the school was going to be shut down, and although Alan's students had always been asexual creatures to him, he was mired in a four-day drunk, and she had great legs, legs like a track star, legs that could wrap around his body twice, the taste and color of warm honey, not that that was an excuse, but on that day his blood pressure rose and his head swam and he felt a warm tingle down in his groin that he hadn't felt in years. She peered up at him and though she didn't fight his touch, she didn't welcome it either. She slipped her arms through her shirt and covered her breasts with her hands, and as he went to touch them, he knew he should stop, that what he was doing was wrong, but he couldn't—it just felt so right.

Alan shrugged. "School," he said. "She was having problems in history class and wanted to know if I could recommend a tutor."

"Nothing else?"

Alan shook his head.

"She didn't follow you out into the parking lot? You didn't take her somewhere?"

"Jesus, Jeff. No."

The sheriff plucked tobacco from his tongue and rubbed it in between his fingers, smudging the tips a juicy black. "Sure, sure," he said. "I, for one, believe you. There's just the rumors and all. The fact that you were nowhere to be found. That you might've been the last person who spoke with her. That when you did find out she was missing, you didn't come give a statement voluntarily. All strange, Mr. Donahue. I think it was you who taught me that if it quacks like a duck, walks like a duck, then it's a duck."

"I don't remember teaching you that at all. It was history class, if you remember."

"Might've been someone else. High school's all a blur now." He grinned a yellow-stained grin. He slapped his knees and leaned forward and stood. "Well," he said. "If you think of anything…"

"Certainly," Alan said. He pointed to where the door should've been.


ALAN TOOK TO DRINKING MORE than he should have, though he didn't blame himself considering the circumstances: his school shutting down, impending joblessness, Amber. It was her that troubled him the most. He couldn't stop thinking about her. It got to the point he was even dreaming about her. The one he had most often, they were sitting in the bed of a pickup out by

Bluestem Lake, this brown and murky reservoir in Osage County, and they cuddled like lovers and looked up at the stars. Soon, they began to make out, and she started to pant, and he could feel his blood pressure rise, feel himself getting aroused. She would pull away from him and smile and open her mouth up as wide as she could. She would then start to pull out her teeth, one by one, until all she had left were these bloody, pockmarked gums, hands filled with red-stained teeth. He would wake up screaming, and he briefly thought he needed to go see someone, a doctor, a therapist, somebody, but he knew that wouldn't help—only seeing her again would.

So he volunteered for the search party. Amber's father was there, and when Alan showed, he stared at him suspiciously, no doubt having heard the rumors: the sexual trysts, the unlawful humping in the dark library, the theory that he'd strangled her so she'd keep her mouth shut. Amber's father gave the police a sweater she'd often worn, an ugly little thing that caused the dogs to bark in anticipation once they'd gotten a whiff. They started at the IGA and then walked east down the highway, calling out Amber's name every few yards. Of course, no one answered back. The search party sauntered behind the dogs, seemingly resigned to the fact this search would be fruitless like all the rest. Even Amber's father appeared hopeless. His face was long and bruised and yellowed, like he hadn't slept in weeks, but he trudged forward, perhaps convinced that they'd find her alive any minute, perhaps all hope gone and merely searching out of obligation. Alan wouldn't have been surprised either way. It had been weeks since she'd gone missing, and the police didn't have any leads. But people believed what they believed, oftentimes despite the overwhelming evidence to the contrary.

After a few miles, they came up on a dirt road cut out from the tree line. It looked like it had hardly been used. A fallen tree blocked the entrance, and a rusted gate had been pulled back. It was now warped and oxidized to the point of disrepair. The dogs stopped in front of it, sniffing the air, and then barreled down the trail. About two hundred yards down the dirt road, the dogs stopped again. They barked and they howled and they pointed west toward the woods. It was dark in there, the underbrush thick and dense. They all stared for a few moments, the dogs barking, the woods, however, silent. Only a stiff breeze could be heard, blowing above the canopy.

"Amber!" her dad yelled. "Amber, are you out there?"

Not even an echo answered back.

The deputies let loose the dogs and followed behind, sprinting through the underbrush. Soon, they came upon the smell. It was putrid, debilitating even, something that Alan would never be able to forget. It was like it crawled up his nose. Like it got right up inside him and twisted his guts. One man stopped and began to vomit. Another started to gag but kept running. Amber's father just wailed.

They found her in a little clearing. She was naked, and she was tied to a post, her wrists shackled with a rope. She had been there a while and was hardly recognizable anymore. What remained was just dried tissue and muscle and blood, the color and texture of beef jerky. Maggots crawled over her, and flies shrouded her skull. A coyote or a wild dog had eaten her eyes and face. Around her was a collection of bones. Leg bones, it looked like, from cows and deer. Tied to the post above her head was a bison skull. On her stomach was a picture of a small person, drawn in her own blood.

EVENTUALLY THE LAST DAY OF school, for the year and for the town forever, came. Hardly anyone showed. Maybe ten or twelve students. Susan was there. Blinky was there. Ms. Redtree, along with dozens of covered wagons fashioned from Radio Flyers and bed sheets. Ms. Redtree lined each of the wagons up in a row behind a black line she'd spray-painted onto the red clay. There were about thirty or so parcels of land marked out by hula-hoops and wooden rods lodged into the soil. These represented the 160 acres the settlers could claim as their own. Several had flags draped from the top, the ones that had already been staked out by the Sooners, the settlers who had entered the territory illegally and hidden out before the Land Run officially opened on April 22, 1889.

It had started at high noon that day. An estimated 50,000 settlers lined up to take part. People who had decided to start anew someplace else, who had, for whatever reason, decided to abandon their birthplaces for the promises of the West. A fitting tribute to the end of the school year, Alan thought. The underclassmen would start a new school come next fall. The teachers and administrators, like Ms. Redtree and himself, would be forced to find employment in other districts or new professions altogether. Most of them would be unqualified for anything else and be forced to take jobs they hadn't worked since college, delivering pizzas or assisting a plumber. Honest work. Work that they shouldn't, but would nonetheless, be ashamed of. It took a lot of courage to do a thing like that. And it wasn't a normal kind of courage. Not the kind where people acted on impulse, running into a burning building to save a child or to shield a friend from a grenade. This took forethought, a premeditated and detailed plan, execution. It was a type of courage Alan was afraid he didn't have.

To start the reenactment, Ms. Redtree fired a cap gun into the air. A little burst of smoke spewed from the barrel, and the children loafed out of the starting gate. They didn't rush or fight over the parcels of land. Instead, they malingered, dragging the wagons behind them and shielding their eyes from the harsh summer sun. Ms. Redtree slouched in disappointment at their obvious disinterest. Alan wasn't surprised. Here these kids were, following orders because they didn't know they no longer had to. As of three o'clock, when Ms. Redtree had fired the cap gun, the Pawhuska school system no longer existed, and along with its dissolution, he and she were stripped of their power. But here they were, Alan and Blinky and Ms. Redtree and all the kids, pulling red wagons and claiming imaginary land stripped from its rightful, imaginary owners, afraid that if they disobeyed, the Little People would come, and take from them all that they held dear.

# The Motion of Bodies

IT WAS JUST A TWEET, AFTER ALL, A FIF-
TY-NINE-CHARACTER JOKE HE'D TYPED BEFORE GETTING ON THE
plane in Miami: "On my way to the USVI, hope I don't get Ebola JK I'm white." But by the time he landed several hours later,
refreshed from a Scotch-induced nap, he'd already received six
voicemails from his sister, the last one stating ominously, "I am so
sorry this is happening to you."

The airport in St. Thomas was unlike any Harry'd been to before. The plane touched down, idled along the runway, then parked
upon the tarmac, and he and the other passengers deplaned and
stretched under the piercing sunlight. Airline employees greeted
them with their luggage and a complimentary bushwhacker, a
sweet drink light on the rum, and as Harry drank it he wondered
what exactly his sister had meant. She'd made it quite known she
didn't approve of his adopting a child, a single man, a solitary man,
a man, she feared, who might be gay. Her disapproval had hurt; he
couldn't lie to himself that it didn't, but it hardly mattered. For the
longest time he'd felt he wasn't in control of his life, at the whim
of some unnamed cosmological force, like a particle accelerated at

near light speed, destined to collide with countless other particles in a barrage of energy equal to a million atomic bombs, but now all that would change—he would be a father, the one thing he wholly desired before anything else. He would love and care for and mold a beautiful little girl, and he could take solace in that fact: he would affect her, whatever that was worth, good or bad.

But, he thought as he waved down a taxi, that couldn't be it. Sadie had eventually come around, at least out loud she did, and congratulated him, in fact, taking him out as if they were in college again, just searching for an excuse to get drunk enough to sing Don McLean at the top of their lungs, and so he tried to discard it and enjoy the moment. It was a beautiful island, despite the recent hurricane. It wasn't so much the white beaches and blue skies, but it was the dichotomy of it all. There were boarded up shacks next to a Bvlgari shopping center, a villa next to a man with a goat, selling mangos and pineapple on the roadside. Condominiums without roofs and boarded windows sprawled up the mountainside. Trees had been uprooted, dirt and debris piled aside the highway, victims picking through what remained. The rich, however, didn't seem as affected. Their property was already under repair, heavy machinery parked next to towering mansions and high-end retail centers. There didn't seem to be a middle class here, only the super rich and the dirt poor, and this, for some reason Harry couldn't quite articulate, intrigued him—it was like witnessing particles and anti-particles in a quantum element, at once quintessential to the others' survival, but forever repelling each other with their unlike charges.

"I know you," the cabby said, pointing up at the rear-view mirror, his finger bobbing up and down like he was scolding Harry.

"You ever been to Oklahoma City?" Harry asked, sure the man had not. Harry just had that type of face—roundish, cheery, pink-cheeked—so that he was often stopped on the street, his interrogator wondering how she knew him.

"No, no," the man said. "I saw you on the news, my man. Picture blown up everywhere." The man had a thick Caribbean accent, and so Harry had trouble understanding him, but he thought the man was mistaking for a news anchor.

"No," Harry said, waving his open palms in front of him, "I'm not famous or anything. Just a lowly physics professor. I teach classical mechanics to community college students."

"No, no. You are famous. You are. But where did I see you?" The man stroked his goatee as he pulled into the resort where Harry would be staying. It was a nice place, sprawling rather than vertical, plastered in multi-colored stucco. It resembled a child's toy in that regard—bright pink and lime green—and everywhere guests meandered about with drinks in their hands, all of them smiling, smiling, smiling, and Harry thought: *Yes. This is exactly what I need.*

The man parked. When Harry turned around to square up the fee with him, though, the man had lost his smile. For a moment, Harry was confused—why did the cabbie look so angry?—but he didn't have time to consider the man's outrage. The driver simply punched Harry right in the nose, and before everything went black, Harry could've sworn he heard the bone snap.

THE HOSPITAL, IT TURNED OUT, was nice. It was clean and bright and smelled of chemicals, just like any hospital stateside. Before his trip it wasn't like Harry had considered what a hospital in the US Virgin Islands would be like; however, he found himself surprised that this was so. For some reason he'd just figured the facilities he took for granted back home—hospitals, city streets, metro bus terminals—would be dated and dingy, like visiting a third world country. He scolded himself for this impulse, finding it, well, racist, but it was still there, nagging at him like a canker sore he couldn't keep from flicking with his tongue.

His doctor was a young man, early thirties Harry guessed, and it was he who finally broke the news to Harry. "Four hundred and fifty thousand retweets between taking off and landing. A million more during your cab ride and here at the hospital. You've been on CNN, MSNBC, Fox News. You name it. That is the very definition of going viral."

"That wasn't my intent," Harry said. "It really wasn't. I'm not racist."

The doctor flattened his lips. He was trying to remain neutral, neither affirming nor denying Harry's statement. How very diplomatic of him, Harry thought.

"I'm sure it'll pass," the doctor said as he tilted Harry's face up by placing two fingers underneath his chin. "You're just the flavor of the week. Everyone will be distracted by some other outrage by next Tuesday. You'll see."

Harry wasn't comforted by the doctor's assertions. The nurses and orderlies and doctors all leered at him, hesitant to engage lest they couldn't control their outbursts. Harry could tell by the way they held their shoulders perched up near their jawlines, like if they got too close, they wouldn't be able to stop from placing their hands on Harry's neck, pressing their thumbs into that soft spot above the sternum until they heard it pop. Despite this, though, Harry hoped the doctor was right. It was a joke, after all, and there were so many more important things going on in the world besides his ill-advised humor, but all hope dissipated when Harry made it back to his hotel room. He was hesitant to log back onto Twitter, but he did, slowly opening his laptop and typing out his password with only his pointer fingers.

"I hope you get raped."

"You bigoted, Nazi scum."

"Better watch your back, motherfucker."

"We are going to ruin your life."

The response went on and on and on, tens upon tens of thousands of them. Harry scrolled downward, thinking he would see an end to the vitriol, but there wasn't, the little blue bar barely having moved on the side of his monitor, the words now flashing by illegibly. It was overwhelming, and Harry couldn't help but feel dizzy, pleading silently to no one in particular, to everyone all at once, *I'm sorry. I didn't mean it. You have to believe me. I really, really didn't.*

HARRY WANTED TO STAY IN bed. He didn't wish to watch television, or turn on his phone, or go online. He only wanted to order room service, direct the concierge to leave the food outside his room, and to charge the bill to his credit card. Lock himself up until his credit line was maxed out, or management kicked him out, one or the other. He would become comfortable in his new life here. He could see the beach from his window, and he'd read mystery novels and meditate. He'd never have to return home, never have to face another person again—the judgment from strangers, their all-too-human sneer that would cut through Harry like nuclear fission.

But he couldn't. He'd come here to adopt his child, and he couldn't hide from her like he had his problems his entire life. Until they ebbed away on their own, or at least until enough people had forgotten so he could reemerge without the shame he'd felt for his mistakes, for drinking too much or for offensive comments, for inappropriate touching and desires and fantasies of taken men. And so, despite the pain and fear and anxiety he thought might cripple him, he left the resort to go to the adoption agency, to see his daughter, about whom he had dreamt for so many nights.

He still had a bandage over his nose, a piece of plaster and gauze strategically placed to hold the bones in place as they healed. Because of the discomfort, the light as he exited the resort was unbearable. Pain shot through his corneas to his cerebral cortex so that he had to shut his eyes and hold his palms against his forehead, but it soon subsided enough for him to make it to the beach. It was calm there, the melodious surf the only noise. Harry dipped his toes into the water and welcomed the sunshine against his neck and bare arms. For the first time since landing, Harry felt relaxed, his worries and anxieties and fears seeping out of him through his outstretched fingertips.

It was then Harry decided he could reattach himself to the world. He pulled out his iPhone, the screen illuminating in that familiar, comforting way, and loaded up Twitter. At first, he only noticed his timeline, updates from Politico and NASA and *The Wall Street Journal*, but at the bottom of his screen was a little pop-up alerting him to his 1,349,735 notifications, and counting. He checked Facebook. The same there—countless messages threatening his safety, his life, the wellbeing of the ones he loved. He had voicemails, dozens upon dozens, from his parents in Phoenix and his boss back in Oklahoma City, from friends, both current and lost, even some he hadn't seen since his twenty-year high school reunion. He ignored them all and pulled up Google Maps, entering the address for the adoption agency. It wasn't far, and so Harry decided he would rather walk than take a cab. He needed the endorphins, a rush of blood and serotonin to make him feel better.

The topography of the island was much different than back home. Instead of red clay and Indian-grass plains stretching out in every direction, Harry's line of sight was constantly changing. To the east churned the Caribbean Sea, deep and crystalline blue, capped by white waves pushed to shore by the seasonal trade winds. Directly in front of him was a winding and rolling highway, and to the west grew a dense tropical forest, elevating against a graphite-colored mountainside, interspersed with brilliant orange and yellow and green flowers. The fauna blended into the landscape, camouflaged by eons of evolution, but when he looked closely, he found an iguana baking in the equatorial sun, and in the tree line Harry could've sworn he spotted a white-tailed deer, but that couldn't be right. Could it?

After an hour's trek, he made it to the adoption agency, a wooden shack nestled into the mountain far from any tourist destination. Chickens roamed around an open dumpster, pecking at bits of refuse that had fallen shy of their destination. By the time he arrived, Harry was exhausted, drenched in sweat, ankle swollen and likely sprained. His nose ached, shooting pain through his cheekbones and sinuses and forehead so that it felt as if his brain might explode. He tried to compose himself the best he could, but he knew he looked like he'd been in a car accident, a homeless man, a desperate man.

*Well*, he thought. *If the shoe fits.*

He walked through the entrance, and it wasn't at all what he'd expected. After the hurricane had hit, orphaning so many children, he'd expected the state agencies to be overwhelmed with need, resources spread thin and conditions unbearable. Images came to him of Katrina years before, news reports of riots in the Big Easy, police sniping looters from the roofs of Target Superstores. This place, however, was clean and well managed. He entered a large room that seemed to double as a welcoming lobby and arts-and-crafts center. Adults showed dozens of children how to make macaroni necklaces as a woman behind a desk eyed him suspiciously.

"Can I help you, mister?" she asked, the "i" pronounced long and like an "e," pulling the word out like *meeeester*. The accent, as much as Harry didn't want to admit it, sounded like the whine of a spoiled toddler.

"Name is Harry Humboldt," he said. "I'm supposed to meet my daughter today."

Her eyes alighted with recognition, and alarm, and she reached for her phone. She dialed four numbers, a colleague's direct extension, and whispered into the receiver, and as she did so, Harry's stomach filled with dread, acid and bile brewing in his lower intestine so that he felt nauseated and dense.

"Ms. Alex will be with you in one meeenute," the woman said as she pretended to busy herself with files.

Ms. Alex showed in less than one minute. She was a heavyset woman, pear-shaped and bulldog-cheeked. Right away Harry didn't like her, and it wasn't so much the bureaucratic way she ushered him into her office, shooing him from contact with impressionable children, but more of a gut feeling—this woman hated him. With every fiber of her being, she loathed everything that was Harry Humboldt.

Her office was small but organized, everything color-coded and in its place. She bid Harry sit with a flick of her wrist, as if she was used to dutiful obedience without even uttering a word.

"I have First Amendment rights," Harry said, preempting how he was sure this conversation was to go. "It was a stupid tweet. It was. It was an even worse joke, but I do have rights."

"Of course you do," Ms. Alex said. "But we don't see this as a First Amendment issue."

"Sure it is. I tweeted something offensive. It's gone viral, and now—"

"This is a safety issue, Mr. Humboldt. We have legitimate concerns about Gloria's safety."

"That is insane," Harry said. "I would never hurt Gloria. I love her. I have wanted nothing more than to be a father."

Ms. Alex turned to her computer and put on reading glasses. " 'I will slit your throat in your sleep.' 'I will set your house on fire.' 'Your children will be murdered as you watch.' 'You're dead, you racist demon.' 'Everyone you love is going to be killed.' This is just a very small portion of what we found online."

Harry swallowed, or tried to. His saliva had all dried up.

"These sound like very real threats of violence," Ms. Alex said.

"They're internet trolls. It'll pass. Surely, it'll all die down."

She pointed at Harry's face. "But for now," she said, "it's manifesting itself quite literally."

"Oh this," Harry said, trying to come up with an excuse that sounded legitimate, "this is nothing. I—uh—well, it's sort of embarrassing."

Ms. Alex stared.

"It was an accident, is all," Harry said. "I fell while getting out of the plane. Face full of cement."

"That's the story you're going with?"

"It's what happened."

"Sure," she said, her tone indicating she remained unconvinced. "It still doesn't change the reality of the matter."

"Which is?"

"I decide if Gloria goes home with you. And I can't, in good conscience, allow that to happen."

Time, to Harry, sped up. He hardly remembered leaving the adoption agency, the moments blurred together into an endless barrage of snapshots, like a drunk trying to piece together memories of the night before: Harry standing, something guttural building inside of him, fuming from his central core; him yelling at Ms. Alex, at no one in particular; a big, muscular man placing him in a chokehold, his arm bent backward, pulled to an impossible angle so that he feared it would break. But it didn't. He was lifted and carried and thrown outside, and he remembered getting up. And he remembered walking, but it wasn't until many hours later he came back to, his face and lips and neck and arms sunburnt, his throat cracked and his head thumping from dehydration. He couldn't speak. He could hardly move. He was just in pain. Every single inch of him ached.

And he knew—he just needed one thing: a drink.

So he made his way to the beach bar. He slathered on SPF 100 and put on a hat and sunglasses and linen pants and went to drown himself in tequila. He ordered a margarita, drank that, drank another, and followed that up with a shot. He sucked lime juice until his mouth puckered and his eyes burned, and the entire time he couldn't help but think that it was a beautiful island. It was, and he should, he decided, enjoy himself.

There was a man there. He was alone and he was balding and he drank a piña colada like he didn't drink all that often, small sips out of a colorful straw. He stared at the ocean and pretended to read a three-week-old *Wall Street Journal*. He looked like a banker. He had the seriousness around the eyes, beady and pointed and hot like an oven, and it wasn't long before Harry started to feel that familiar tingle down in his groin, his inhibitions lowering, like air released from a tire. He would do something stupid, and he didn't want to stop it.

He ordered the man a drink, another piña colada, double rum, and took a seat next to him.

"Alone?" Harry asked.

The man eyed him. He made quick judgments. Intentions. Threats. Inventoried his exits and options. Harry could tell by the way he didn't blink, just took him all in, head to toes to knees. And he liked what he saw. He did. He had this look in his eyes, this glint, like a toddler eying cake for the very first time. The man wasn't gay, or at least that's what he said.

"Just got divorced. Came down here to unwind. Let loose. Hell, who knows? Even meet someone new."

But it was repressed. After two piña coladas, three, twirling the pink umbrella between thumb and forefinger, the man, Tom was his name, began to laugh and tilt his head back and graze his fingers against Harry's forearm. It wasn't long until they had a nightcap back in Harry's room, a sunset. A dip in the hot tub turned into them naked and Harry scooting in behind him, both sweating and sweating and groaning and wincing and Tom saying slow, slow, please, just a little slower, I've never done anything like this before.

But Harry didn't slow.

He sped up.

He pounded.

Harder.

Faster.

Harder.

Until the man screamed. Then there was blood. There was blood and screaming and the man pushed him away, told Harry not to touch him, that he would kill him if he ever told anyone what had happened, and Harry collapsed in the corner. There was blood and shit all over him and he couldn't catch his breath. No matter how hard he tried he couldn't. He just gasped and gasped and fought for a little bit of air, and he knew, down to a cellular level he knew, nothing would ever make any of this right.

HARRY DECIDED TO STAY. HE had nothing back home, really. One of the several hundred voicemails he'd received was from his boss, telling him not to return, that he would ship Harry's personal belongings to the address they had on file, that it would be safer for everyone involved. His friends wouldn't return his calls, treating him as a pariah, their association with Harry deemed bad business, even deleting him on Facebook and Twitter, his total number of friends and followers dwindling from the thousands to the hundreds to the dozens. His sister would take his calls, the only one, but she just seemed to pity him. "Oh, Harry," she'd say. "Oh, honey. Oh, sweetie. I am so, so sorry."

And so he stayed. He rented a bungalow on the beach, no

a/c, no running water, just a floor and a roof and four walls, and he took a job as a bartender serving overpriced rum punches to lawyers on vacation, their foreheads blistered from wearing too little sunscreen. He grew a beard and wore a straw hat so people wouldn't recognize him. He went swimming most days, paddling as far as he could, until his shoulders gave out and his legs cramped up, and he'd turn on his back and let the surf push him back to shore. If he made it, great—he just collected his things and went home and stared at the wall of his hut—but, if one day he didn't, that would be okay, too, he supposed.

Every week Harry hiked to the adoption agency to see Gloria grow up. And she did, quickly. From crawling to walking to talking to wearing bright orange glasses the color of road-construction signs. She played outside in the mornings, oftentimes without direct adult supervision. They would be inside someplace, watching the babies chew ancient action figures, while Harry meanwhile plotted their routines. The younger of the two attendants was named Kary and she waddled and ate York Peppermint Patties and used British slang such as *bollocks*, and the older was named Beatrice and she snorted every time Kary said something.

"I need to go to the loo," Kary'd say, and Beatrice would snort, then return to reading a magazine.

Sometimes, when Kary was away for a while, Beatrice would sneak around the corner to smoke a cigarette. It was against the law to smoke on government property, and so she'd hide behind some bushes, and Harry knew this would be his chance. It would be these few minutes he could grab Gloria and make a run for it.

And so he planned, and he saved. He bought a beat-down Toyota for $800 and two plane tickets to Croatia, which, Harry considered, fit nicely in that sweet spot between too poor to be safe and too expensive to live. It was 1.2 miles from the adoption agency to the airport, which didn't seem too far, but in island traffic that 1.2 miles could take half an hour to traverse. He'd have to pick a day when a cruise ship wasn't scheduled to dock, and he could avoid the dozens of taxis that herded sunburnt tourists up to Mountaintop or Magen's Bay. He got his chance one Thursday morning when the sun wasn't shining and it rained in a way that reminded him of playing under a sprinkler as a child.

He lay across the road in the underbrush, wearing a tool belt equipped with wire cutters, and watched Kary and Beatrice supervise the children. About a dozen or so kids played under the awning, fatherless and motherless kids, kids who had been orphaned long before they knew what the word meant, sucking on their fingers and eating insects and just happy because they knew no different. It wasn't a bad life, Harry supposed. It wasn't great, but it could be worse.

Gloria was near the fence closest to Harry, and she played with another little girl. They each had a toy plastic truck and smashed them into each other, mimicking a car crash. Harry could see their mouths move, forming into wide O's, cheeks ballooned out to make exploding noises, but Harry couldn't hear them over the rain. It was almost deafening, splashing against elephant-ear leaves and pavement, and, for a moment there, Harry found himself daydreaming, imagining it might be best if he gave up this stupid endeavor. He could slink back to the mainland, go about his business as quietly as possible, take a job as a janitor somewhere, as a mail courier, or a barista, someone who just blended into the background, a man without a face or a name, just a product or service. He'd be the coffee guy or the mail guy or the cleaning guy, not the guy who had become a symbol of white privilege and systemic, twenty-first-century entitlement, of the ongoing disease of institutionalized racism, and he might find a semblance of contentment in anonymity. But this thought soon passed when both Beatrice and Kary disappeared.

Harry pulled the hood over his head and hurried. He walked with purpose across the highway and stopped by the fence. Gloria and the other little girl peered up at him, and he put a finger against his lips. They didn't make a sound. They just held onto their toy cars and peered up at him with eyes like marbles.

"Hi," Harry said, and stuck his fingers through the chain-link fence. Gloria looked at him as if in deep concentration, wondering just what to make of these fingers reaching out toward her. "Step back, okay? This will only take a second."

Harry clipped the fence with his wire cutters. He'd thought it would be difficult to shear through the metal, but his cutters were sharp and it only took him about a minute to cut a hole large enough for Gloria to scurry through, and as he worked, the two little girls kept staring at him, completely unafraid, not crying, not fleeing this stranger who was coming through the fence that had kept them safe and secure and inside for the entirety of their lives, and Harry couldn't help but be a little worried about this. Their fight-or-flight instinct conditioned out of them, millions of years of evolution gone as if it was the inevitable result of a life orphaned.

"Would you like to come with me?" Harry asked Gloria, and again she simply blinked at him.

But then he heard rustling; it was Beatrice. She must've been done with her smoke, so Harry grabbed Gloria. He picked her up and held her so close he could feel her heartbeat quicken right before she burst into a torrential, ear-piercing cry. It was so loud and so sudden it startled Harry. She'd been calm just a second ago, but now she wailed. For a second there, Harry thought he should put her down. Maybe hold her. Do something just to let her know that everything, if she gave it a try, would be okay.

But he didn't have time. Beatrice barreled out from behind the tree and spotted him. And so he did the only thing that occurred to him—he ran. He ran back across the street and into the jungle. He ran past trees and lizards, and branches scratched at his face, or maybe it was Gloria, he couldn't tell. But he ran and ran and ran until a side-splitting pain threatened to tear him apart and he burst into a clearing where his little Toyota waited for him, idling.

In the distance, he heard police sirens getting louder, and Gloria continued to wail, now with tiny red scratches covering her cheeks and foliage stuck in her hair. But she was okay. She'd live, and so he placed Gloria in the car seat, careful to buckle her in properly, the latch up near her armpits, the straps secure and tight. He then put the car into gear and drove off as inconspicuously as possible, five miles below the speed limit, always, always using his turn signal. He only got around one turn, however, when he noticed the police cruisers. There were six of them, and they blocked the road. They faced east and Harry west, toward the airport where his plane was waiting for him, flying to Miami to New York to Croatia, and in the back sat Gloria, crying.

He put the car in park and placed his hands on the wheel so they could be seen through the windshield. Several cops exited their cruisers, took shelter behind their open doors, and aimed their firearms. They wouldn't shoot, though. Not with Gloria in the backseat. Harry was certain of that. And so he stayed in the car. Gloria cried. The cops pointed their weapons at him. And Harry put the car into first gear and started to inch forward. The speedometer needle crawled upward. Three miles per hour. Five. Ten. And he coasted toward them, slowly picking up speed. The police warned him to stop. Over a megaphone, a voice ordered him to stop the car, to exit with his hands raised, and to lie face down on the ground. But Harry knew he wouldn't. He let off the gas pedal, took his hands off the wheel, and the car careened down the mountain now, the foliage speeding past in a green blur as he gave in to his own intrinsic inertia. It was freeing in a sense—he was a frictionless ball of mass, no longer at the whim of forces beyond his control—and, for a moment there, he felt at peace. He knew, no matter what, he'd never be able to stop.

# The Deep Down Bone of Desire

IT WAS A TYPICAL THURSDAY MORNING
WHEN SARA PASSED IT: THE VON MAUR'S DISPLAY WINDOW, RE-
plete with mannequins enjoying a holiday scene, and at first she
simply disregarded it—a retail store advertisement, nothing else—
but when Huxley pointed up at the window and said, "Daddy,"
she had to look. The mannequin itself, of course, looked nothing
like Daddy. The plastic was lifeless and its hue chalky. Its rigid
joints bent at awkward angles. But there was, if Sara squinted her
eyes and let them get all blurry, something about it that reminded
her of her husband of twelve years. Perhaps it was the snowflake-
covered sweater it sported, one her husband would wear ironically
to a winter company party, or perhaps it was the sly upturned grin
of its lifeless lips, but it just seemed so oddly familiar. And this
feeling, uncanny as it was, unnerved Sara—there was something
inexplicably off about the whole damn thing.

For instance, the child in the scene—young, gleeful, rosy-
cheeked—did also resemble, in the slightest way, of course, if Sara
looked in just the right angle out her periphery, Hux. There were
differences, obviously. Sara had recently chopped short Hux's long

bangs despite her embarrassing temper tantrum thrown right in the middle of the salon, and the mannequin in the display still had hers, lining her eyes in that off-putting, grown-up sort of way that had irked Sara to no end. But, beyond that, Sara could've sworn Hux had that same exact pair of pajamas: pink with puppy dog prints. Hux had outgrown them a few months prior, and they remained pushed up in a ball in the back of her dresser drawer, a constant and nagging reminder that Sara needed to organize and de-clutter her life, just one more thing that needed to be done.

And then there was the mother in the scene, nursing a white coffee mug. She was off to the side, leaning against a white, non-descript sofa. She wore white leggings and a white T-shirt. She was the only thing in the scene that wasn't splashed with color so that she stood out as this bright, glaring eyesore. And, if she was absolutely honest with herself, and more and more lately Sara had been, this was how she often felt in her own life: she stood out as someone who did not fit. She was like the child's game played in preschool, melodically taught to toddlers to discard the thing that was different, and despite willing herself not to let it, the little tune got stuck in her head: "One of these things is not like the others / One of these things just doesn't belong."

"Can we go in, Mommy?" Hux pulled on Sara's pant leg. "Please please please!"

Later, Sara would like to think it was Hux's insistence that took her into the store, that she had nagged and begged and Sara had relented just to keep her from throwing her umpteenth tantrum of the day, but that was a lie. She was drawn to the store, too, the display acting as some sort of tractor beam, pulling her inside. The store itself was bright and huge and filled with holiday cheer, the soft hum of Jingle Bell jazz, the thrum of shoppers' laughter. As soon as Sara walked through the doors, it was like she was a child again, enthralled by the rapture of the holiday season. She wandered down the aisles in awe, mentally checking off her wish list: a pair of heels here, some diamond earrings there. The necklaces caught her attention, so sparkly and enticing, and so did the hats, the floppier the better. She knew, however, that Daryl would not buy her anything like that for Christmas. Since having Hux, their gift giving had turned practical instead of romantic, a set of radial tires or air filters, cutlery or new smoke detectors. Things that were needed, not necessarily wanted. And Sara had been fine with that. She didn't expect life to be some sort of never-ending rom-com, but she did hope that every once in a while, not even that often, just like once or twice a year, really, Daryl would surprise her with something, a nice little clutch or even just a Starbucks gift card. Just a small little knickknack that said he still gave a damn. He didn't, and that was okay, she supposed, but that didn't mean she couldn't—rarely of course—spoil herself. That was when she saw it: a purse. It was a Kate Spade, this cute little thing with the strap and the leather and that feeling only a new bag could bring, and she decided she shouldn't feel bad if she bought something just this once. It was, after all, just one little thing.

SARA CARRIED HER PURSE EVERYWHERE she went after
that: to the DMV to renew her driver's license; to Aldi to grab a
bag of avocados and pre-made, individually wrapped peanut but-
ter and jelly sandwiches; to Hux's dance recitals. Everywhere she
went, other mothers would stop her and ask, "Where did you get
that bag? Where? Where can I get one of my own?" And the entire time, Sara couldn't help but feel like she was floating. It was
enchanting in a way, like how she'd felt the first time boys had noticed her, when she had been sixteen and her older cousin's friend
had handed her a room-temperature Coors Light and said, "Here,
cutie. Take a load off." She felt empowered. She felt, and she was
embarrassed to admit this, unstoppable.

She scolded herself for this feeling. It was so, well, superfi-
cial. She hated it. She had, in her younger days, even chided her
mother and sisters and other girls at school for overvaluing material things, their socioeconomic status, but here she stood, right in
the middle of T-ball signups, hoping beyond hope someone would
stop her and tell her again just how beautiful her bag was.

But nobody did.

They didn't say a word.

And so Sara wondered why. She stood there in line, dozens
of other mothers standing around, carrying on about Betsy and
how everyone thought she was perhaps letting herself go and how
jealous they were of Ann for finding herself on that mission trip
to Haiti, and wondered why no one even gave her bag a second
glance. It still looked good. The leather still had that new sheen
and that just-brought-home-from-the-department-store smell. It

was still in fashion, this year's design in fact, and it went perfectly well with her teal-green flats and her pants. Well, not so much with the pants. They were a little worn and faded, having been bought…well, she couldn't exactly remember when she'd bought them. And they did have a string curling away from the pocket, so Sara tried to grab it without the other mothers noticing and rip it off, the whole time nodding, *yes, yes, of course Ann looks ten years younger, more in fact,* and tried not to rip a hole down the seam. And she was able to. It was easy enough. But then she had to hold on to the string, keep it in her hand, rubbing it between her coarse fingertips, and she knew, deep down in her bones she knew, she had to replace her pants before the day's end.

By the time she and Hux got back to Von Maur, the display window had changed. It was still a family scene, still a mother and husband and daughter, but instead of the parents watching the little girl opening Christmas presents, they huddled together around a dining room table. The father and the daughter sat there, the husband's hands clasped together as if in prayer, and the daughter spooning an invisible dinner into her open, waiting mouth, and Sara couldn't help but think that this was them, this was Daryl and Hux and she at last year's Christmas dinner. Maybe she was going crazy—she certainly felt a little crazy—but it was like she remembered this exact moment. Sara had been standing over the turkey, trying to carve it, while Daryl criticized her technique, telling her how to hold the knife and the double-tined prongs, explaining that her angle was all wrong and that she would tear the meat and hit bone and dull the knife, and she'd argued with him. She told him to keep his mouth shut, that she'd been feeding this family for years, thank you very much, without much input from him, and no, game-day burgers on the grill did not count, and that she didn't need his advice now, the whole time Hux staring down at her plate as if she wished she could disappear. Sara felt bad about this later, and still did, in fact, and it didn't help that Daryl had been right— she had hit bone, and the meat was shredded into jagged little cuts—but when Sara entered the store, all this regret and shame and anger she had felt for so long about that day, for fighting in front of Hux and the way she resented Daryl's smugness, all of it seemed to just melt away. She felt whole again. She felt—and this time she wasn't embarrassed to admit it—at home.

THE PURSE TURNED INTO PANTS, and the pants turned into some heels, the heels into a dress. Soon, she'd bought a necklace, and then a day or two later, matching earrings. She bought a blazer and sunglasses and rings and a watch, sneakers and leggings and three or four blouses. When her wardrobe was finished, she decided she needed to redo the house. She bought a new sectional, a couple chaise lounges, even a few bookcases to display her brand new, ceramic knickknacks: little Hindu elephants and dream catchers and Congolese tribal masks, worldly things, things that made her feel more sophisticated, more interesting somehow, as if by just owning them, she could experience a thousand experiences all at once. She knew this to be crazy, of course. She hadn't experienced these things, and she didn't go around telling everyone she had travelled the world or had joined the Peace Corps out of college or had gone on safari with Daryl for their eighth wedding anniversary. She did, however, often daydream about what that would be like, to be a world traveller, to be a woman of the world, and this, these little fantasies, didn't harm anyone. They made her happy, in fact.

Beyond her happiness, Sara had noticed other changes, too. When she stood in line to buy stamps or pick up her dry cleaning or just about anywhere, in fact, people started doing stuff for her. It wasn't all that noticeable at first—she would drop her purse by accident, spilling a tube of ruby red lipstick or a hair clip, and some teenage girl would pop out of nowhere to help her out. She'd be a few cents short while getting her morning Frappuccino, and a middle-aged, rotund man would slide up next to her with a dollar bill. Everywhere she went, people smiled at her and opened doors for her and complimented her on her boots or her nails or her smile, and Sara couldn't help but bask in the attention. She felt like a movie star, if maybe just a B-reel character actress, but still, the people were so nice, just so, so nice, and, even though she felt a little silly about all this, she half expected the paparazzi to be waiting for her out in the parking lot, snapping photographs of little old her, to be published the next morning in *US Weekly*, or, dare she hope, even *People*.

Of course, Daryl started to notice all the new stuff. Each time she came through the front door carrying a couple shopping bags, he would pucker his lips and shake his head disapprovingly, like a father berating a misbehaving child. Well, Sara thought, she wasn't his child. She was his wife, and she was, both by vow and by law, entitled to these things. What was his was hers and vice versa, and it had been twelve good goddamn years, so why shouldn't she spoil herself? She deserved it. When the credit card bill came, however, and Daryl clucked that stupid, little, annoying cluck that he did with his tongue, Sara did, for an instant, feel bad—there were one or two more zeros than she'd anticipated—but the moment soon passed when he opened his idiotic, mushy little mouth.

"I just think maybe it would be wise if we tempered our spending a little bit," he said. "For Hux's sake."

"I'm sorry?"

"I'm just thinking. She's probably due for a growth spurt. She'll need new shoes and dresses and a jacket and stuff. You know, stuff that fits."

The nerve of him!

The absolute, motherfucking—yes, she swore—nerve of him!

For years she had been trying to get him interested in Hux. She'd plead with him to attend parent-teacher conferences, her ballet recitals, to just spend a few minutes after work playing tea party. "But, babe," he'd say, "the big game," or "the big meeting," or "the big whatever." And now, now that she dared do something for herself for a change, he had the gall to open his mouth and invoke their daughter? The one she had just about single-handedly raised since birth?

The motherfucking, hair-splitting, homicidal-raging nerve of that guy!

And so she kept spending. She bought new curtains and new rollerblades and new china and new silverware and new stemware and new wood floors and new showerheads. Everything had to be replaced. She hired contractors to remodel her kitchen and to add a new family room to the back of the house. She bought new beds for Hux's room and the master and even the guest room, despite it only having been used maybe a dozen or so times. She bought workout equipment, a treadmill and Bowflex machine and free weights, and called the contractors back out to add another room to the house, an in-home gymnasium, and soon, and this came as a surprise even to Sara, more people started to notice. Neighbors dropped by to take pictures and the homeowner's association wanted to feature her home in the annual neighborhood garden show and an editor at *Edmond Living* called her and wanted to do a profile of her and her beautiful home. "Just how do you do it?" she asked, and it seemed like everyone came to know her by name. She'd walk down the street, and strangers would call out, "Sara! Sara Jones! Can we take your picture?"

And the craziest thing happened every time she would pass by the Von Maur display window—the mother in the scene just looked happier. She smiled and she beamed and she dominated the scene, the puny little husband now dismissed into the dark, dank little corner, and the woman wore the prettiest red dress, this strapless little thing with a pencil skirt, her head cocked to the side, declaring to the world that she was ready. Whatever life threw at her, she was ready. She was so much happier, in fact, that Sara couldn't help but buy that red dress and wear it home just to see Daryl's stupid face when she walked through the door.

Soon, stuff filled every single room of the house—new, shiny, smile-inducing stuff—and for the first time in a long time, Sara felt happy. Truly, undeniably, cheek-hurting happy. It wasn't long, however, until the phone calls began. The first happened one day after dinner. The family was sitting on the new sectional—this classy, creamy, modern thing Sara had picked up on sale, actually—and watching a movie, the cartoon one where the characters were actually a group of superheroes in hiding, and Sara couldn't help but think that she related to the mother in that movie, to be a superhero all these years and to suffer through life an ordinary, plaid-wearing soccer mom. Well, by God, not anymore.

That was when the phone rang. It was the home phone and not one of their cell phones, so Sara knew it was something important. It wasn't Kathy with the latest extramarital gossip going around the PTA or Chase calling Daryl about tickets to see Rush. Rather, it was probably the school, calling about Hux pooping in another kid's backpack, or maybe even one of their doctors, asking he or she to come into the office first thing in the morning, "as soon as you possibly can, actually." So Daryl and Sara had a stare-off over Hux's head. He gave her the I've-worked-all-fucking-day look, brows arched, mouth puckered like he was eating something sour, and she gave him her best I-always-have-to-deal-with-this-type-of-shit grimace, eyes wide and nostrils flared, like she was on her very last straw, and all the while the phone rang, and rang, and rang.

Finally, the stare-down ended in a stalemate, and Sara's chirpy, recorded voice filled the living area: "Thank you for calling the Joneses. We can't answer your call at the moment, but if you please leave

your name and number, we'll get back to you as soon as we can."
The beep was mostly drowned out by some monsters shooting laser guns to Hux's giggling delight. Because of this, it was difficult for Sara to make out the nasal voice on the other end of the line. It sounded like a Bob Allford or maybe a Tom Vonfeldt, and he was from some company or another, and Sara looked to Daryl for any signs of recognition, but he had none, instead having lost interest and begun perusing the illuminated screen of his iPhone, smirking at some other middle-aged man's snarky comment on Facebook.

Later, when Hux and Daryl had gone to bed, Sara listened to the voice message. It was from a Gary Pewter—she made a mental note to get her hearing checked—and he was from Legacy Bank in town. She googled the company online, and he was in their Securities department. They bought up bad debt from department stores and credit card companies and payday lenders and other banks and then went after the debtors for collection. Gary was actually a vice president, and he had an online profile on the company's "About Us" page. He was bald, with Coke-bottle glasses and an upturned lip like he smelled something putrid. Right away, Sara didn't like him, and it wasn't so much that he looked like a squirrel, but it was because she knew, all the way deep down in her bones she knew, this man wasn't there to help her.

THE BANK, SARA NOTED, SMELLED of mold. She couldn't quite pinpoint the source of the smell, but it was most definitely there, like a soggy ceiling tile, soaked from a leaky roof after a spring thunderstorm. No one else, however, seemed to notice it. Employees and customers alike smiled politely when she and Daryl and Hux walked through the revolving door. A teller greeted them like a hostess might, and Sara jumped when the woman seemed to pop out of nowhere, eyes darty and neck strained like an ostrich.

"Welcome to Legacy Bank," she said. "My name is Kara. How can we assist you today?"

It didn't help that Sara carried a snub-nosed .38 in her handbag. Daryl had gotten it for her years before when concealed carry became legal in the state. Usually, she kept it locked in her closet where Hux couldn't get to it, but she'd grabbed it that morning, along with her license to carry, because of some loosely congealed plan that if things didn't go her way when meeting with Gary Pewter, she would have to do something. What that something was, Sara couldn't bring herself to concretely form in her mind, but she had the gist of it: a purse full of cash and a quick getaway. It was crazy, she knew, and downright stupid—she had a better chance of winning the lottery than pulling off a successful bank heist—but she was also desperate, and, for the first time in her life, happy. She just couldn't dream of letting that slip away.

Kara escorted them to Mr. Pewter's office, a quaint little space adjacent to the teller line, where a squirmy man waited for them. He wasn't what Sara had always pictured a banker to be—slick, double-breasted, smelling of leather—but rather a dork in a polo shirt a size too big for him. And she had been right; she didn't like him—she could tell by the smug way he smiled that all he cared about was making a quick buck, padding the company's bottom line, whomever be damned.

"I sure do appreciate you two taking the time out of your day to come see me," he said. He stood and shook their hands. On his desk sat a placard that read, "Gary Pewter / Serious About Service." He knelt down to Hux's level. "You must be Huxley," he said. "Your father has told me you're about to be six years old. Is that true?"

Hux shied away and grabbed ahold of Sara's leg, resting her head against Sara's handbag, only a thin piece of leather separating her from a loaded gun, and, for a second there, Sara couldn't help but think that maybe, just maybe, she was failing as a mother.

"She's shy," Sara said, and they all took a seat to begin their meeting. Hux sat on her father's lap, and Sara made a mental note that if things went south, she would force Hux underneath Mr. Pewter's desk—she figured that might be the safest spot if bullets started flying.

Mr. Pewter retrieved a file from a desk drawer, one he'd obviously just perused before they'd arrived, and laid it neatly on his desk.

"I know this is a difficult thing to talk about," he said. "And this is never easy, but I want you to know I'm not an unreasonable man, and we aren't an unreasonable bank."

His nasal voice annoyed Sara. It wasn't just the tone—a high-pitched, whiny register—but also because he seemed so sincere, like he was just trying to help someone incapable of helping herself, and it made her want to say *screw it* and reach down into her purse and take out the gun. It was a stupid impulse, she knew, much like buying a pair of sunglasses while in the cash wrap line at Von Maur, but it was there nonetheless, irresistible and strong. She wondered what Mr. Pewter's face would look like when she brandished the weapon, that silvery, small little package of boom. He'd probably pucker up, shoulders shivering, nose scrunched as if holding in a sneeze. His face would be priceless.

"But we are looking at a very large sum, nearly $250,000, and after looking over your financial statement here, it doesn't seem like you have any collateral to pledge."

"The house," Daryl said. "There's got to be equity in it."

"The additions to your home cost more than the value they added. You actually now owe more than the house is worth, I'm afraid."

Sara could see it now—Mr. Pewter would fall from his chair, his petrified eyes locked on her, and cower to the floor. "Hands up," she would tell him. "Get to your feet and grab the vault key. You're gonna need it." She'd jab the barrel of the gun into the small of his back, making his knees buckle from fear, and force him into the crowded lobby, and the whole time she would feel so powerful. So powerful—like a lioness protecting her cubs. *Yes, that's it*, she thought, *I* am *the Queen of the Jungle*.

"Like I said, though," Mr. Pewter said, "We aren't unreasonable. We don't want to own your house. We don't want to repossess your belongings. We're not in the business of selling your personal items, and I'm sure we can come up with some sort of payment plan that would benefit everyone involved."

"What were you thinking?" Daryl asked, leaning forward as if he could just swoop in and save the day, and Sara decided that when she made Mr. Pewter open the vault, she'd make Daryl get inside, too. Yeah. She'd make some lowly teller tie Mr. Pewter and Daryl up in there, dirty socks stuffed into their annoying, know-it-all mouths, eyes duct-taped shut so when they were finally rescued, their eyebrows would be ripped out of their pores, and she would go around handing out money to all the hourly employees and the ripped-off bank customers, fifty dollars here, a hundred there, and they would thank her. They'd say, "Thank you, kind stranger. Thank you, oh, so very much."

"We would, of course, need to have some sort of act in good faith. A down payment, say, something along the lines of five percent of the outstanding balance."

"Twelve thousand dollars?" Daryl asked.

"Twelve thousand, five hundred, actually," Mr. Pewter said.

"We don't have that kind of money," Daryl said. "Not just lying around."

She would then grab Hux and take the car and she would head south. She could be in Mexico in nine hours, just hit the highway and run. She'd be like Bonnie from Bonnie and Clyde. She'd be like Patty Hearst. She'd be Robin Hood.

"Momma," Hux said, tugging on her pant leg, eyes glazed with boredom. "I'm hungry."

But she knew, deep down in her bones she knew, none of that would ever happen. If she did pull out the gun, she wouldn't really know what to do with it. She'd probably be more afraid than Mr.

Pewter even, and when she started waving it around, she'd probably wind up shot dead, in front of her little girl no less, who would forever after be scarred. It was a fantasy, much like the life she had secretly hoped for while young, a teenage girl drunk on romantic comedies and fairy tales. Real life just didn't end up happily ever after, and she knew that. She did. She'd just forgotten it for a little while, or at least ignored it for as long as she could, and now, she knew, it was time for the fantasy to end.

"We'll get you the money," Sara said to that smug-faced prick Gary Pewter. "Don't you fucking worry."


AND SO SARA ACTED QUICKLY. The very next morning, she went down to City Hall and applied to have a garage sale. She felt good about it in fact. The lady who took her application was elderly and purple haired and pink lipped, and just sat there with her arms folded and said the nicest things.

"I just love those sunglasses," she said when Sara approached. "Where on Earth did you get those things?"

"Von Maur," Sara said. "They were having a sale, actually. Picked up three for the price of two."

"That's a steal," the lady said.

"I know," Sara said. "Tell me about it."

As Sara filled out the one-page application, she and the little old lady talked. They talked about the weather and seasonal allergies and the unfortunate events that had transpired down at the post office. "Just terrible," the little old lady said, and even though

Sara hadn't any idea what she was talking about, she nodded along as if she did. "I guess that's why they call it 'going postal.'"

"I bet you're right," Sara said. "Just tragic."

The little old lady smacked her lips and smiled as she took Sara's application. She put on her glasses and scanned the boxes to make sure everything was as it should be, and when she was done, she smiled up at Sara with the whitest teeth Sara had ever seen and said, "You know, I really do like those sunglasses." She winked. "We could, if you were interested of course, if you had something to offer in exchange, say, bump the sale out one more day. Just in case." She smudged out the ending date Sara had written in there and wrote in an extra day, free of charge.

"Thank you," Sara said, taking off her sunglasses and handing them to the old lady. "Thank you, oh, so very much."

The morning of the garage sale, Sara arranged all her for-sale items as best she could. She placed her new blouses and dresses and jackets on old, ugly roll racks and chipped folding tables, and it all looked so wrong. Most of the items weren't but just a few weeks old, but they looked worn and beat up on these old racks and three slightly used mannequins. The mannequins were remarkably lifelike, almost off-puttingly so, like a painted portrait whose eyes follow an observer around a room. There was a mother, a father, and a young daughter, almost identical to the three in the Von Maur display window, and she placed them right in the middle of the lawn, decked out in the finest clothes she'd recently purchased for the family. On the daughter, she put a silky red ballerina dress, covered in frills and sequins. The father she displayed in a brand new, custom-made Tom James tuxedo, single breasted and double buttoned, a handsome three-piecer that, Sara noted, Daryl hadn't bitched about when she brought it home for him. For the mother, she donned a black evening gown, strapless and form fitting and, if she was honest with herself, the most gorgeous and graceful thing she had ever worn. It felt almost evil to be selling it, but, she thought, she had messed up, and now she had to do what was necessary, even if it did feel wrong.

It wasn't long before people started showing up. The shoppers were mostly women, middle-aged housewives with oversized sunglasses and black-dyed hair. They wore dark red lipstick and touched everything—the dresses and the serving trays and appliances, the fur coats and wool scarves and velvet hats. It was as if these women felt entitled to Sara's things, and each time they laid a finger on an item, Sara couldn't help but flinch. These were her things. *Hers.* She had earned them, not these women, not the same bored housewives who had complimented her necklace and pearl earrings while in line to pay gymnastics dues at the YMCA. Not these bourgeois, pompous, child-women masquerading as prudent shoppers nitpicking at Sara's most prized possessions. They were scavengers. Lowly, soul-sucking parasites.

But, she thought, she shouldn't be so hard on these women. They were, if Sara thought about it, so much like herself. They desired nice things, but rarely had the means to splurge on themselves. They made do by buying last year's styles in bargain stores or local consignment shops or estate sales. They would pick up three or four items and carry them around, perusing more, discarding one or two at a time, until finally deciding on a single, solitary item, not even the one they most wanted, but a compromise, one they were used to making at this point, and that was okay. It was just the way life was—an endless barrage of minor compromises that summed up to what could be described as contentment. That was the look these women had as they ambled up one by one to pay for their new blouse or clutch, contentment, and that, Sara decided, wasn't all that bad. It was almost desirable, in fact.

At the end of the day, most of Sara's new things had been picked clean, with only a few stragglers remaining. She hadn't made as much as she'd wanted, but it was enough. They would get to keep their house, though they'd still have years of debt to pay down, but they wouldn't be destitute, which was a win, she supposed. There were a few other pieces still left to sell, not enough to make a dent in that debt, but that was okay. There was an umbrella she'd picked up at Target of all places, this bland, wooden-handled thing, and a candy dish, something she'd bought on a whim. There were also the mannequins, still sporting their evening wear, priced too expensive to sell. Standing in front of them were Hux and Daryl, playing. They seemed happy, smiling and laughing as they arranged the mannequins into poses and then mimicked them, standing lifeless in uncomfortable positions, arms outstretched like Egyptian hieroglyphs, knees buckled so that they half stood, half squatted, and they did a pretty decent job. Other than the difference in dress, they really did look alike, the mannequins and her family—plastic, frozen, scheming—and

Sara had to admit that it could be worse. If she really, deep down thought about it, it could. It could be so, so much worse.

# Rainbow Pennant

IT WAS A SMALL PLACE, A MANUFACTUR-
ER OF PENNANTS AND FLAGS, HOUSED IN A 15,000-SQUARE-FOOT
metal building. In the front was a retail store, banners posted to
corkboard walls, screen-printed sales signs declaring *15% off this
week only*, emblazoned in red, 360-point Tahoma. Out front was
one of those inflatable men, three stories tall, flapping and waving in the breeze, despite the fact walk-in sales only accounted for
about eight percent of gross revenue. It had been Harold's son-in-
law's idea. Craig was a good kid. He really was. A good husband to
Harold's daughter, a good father to Harold's grandchildren, even
if he was a bit slow. Could be worse, Harold thought. She could've
married some guy who moved her to New York or California,
someplace he wouldn't be able to see her and her kids whenever he
wanted. Yeah, he thought, could be much worse.

Harold had dreaded coming into the store that morning, the
first time in decades, really. He knew everyone was going to make
a big deal about his retirement, even though they'd promised they
wouldn't. Sharon, his daughter, would bake a cake. Sugar free so as
not to get his blood sugar too high. There'd be speeches, probably.

Mack, from the printing office, Harold's longest-tenured employee, would probably be corralled into giving one. Harold remembered the day he'd hired Mack, as a pimply faced kid fresh out of the University of Central Oklahoma with a degree in graphic design. Hardworking guy. Loyal. If Harold had his way, he'd be the one taking over Rainbow Pennant, not Craig. But life was like that—there were things that had to be done, and so they were. All you could do then was just hope for the best.

It wasn't long before his employees began to show. Susan arrived first. She'd been with him for six years. During that time, she'd gone through a divorce and put two kids through college. She was a good woman. Strong woman. Determined and smart. She chewed Copenhagen and was a whiz with the equipment, and Harold considered her family. When she walked in, she had tears in her eyes.

"It's not a sad day," he said, partly to comfort her, partly to persuade himself. "It's not."

Then came Buzz, a twenty-year-old kid who worked in the warehouse; Charlotte, who kept the books; and then Mack. He was disappointed, Harold knew, and who could blame him? Harold never thought Mack had assumed he'd get the store one of these days, but maybe he'd hoped Harold would sell it to him, work out some carry-back note and get him set up to put aside a nest egg. Harold would've liked to, that was sure, but it was never said aloud, and he had responsibilities to take care of. The last to show, of course, was Craig, and he was all smiles when he walked in. A salesman by training, he'd worked with the Oklahoma City Thunder prior to coming to work for Harold, selling season-ticket packages to oilmen and bankers. Now he hocked signage and banners and would be, alongside Harold's daughter, the owner of this place.

Despite it being Harold's last day, the store opened as usual. Susan powered up the registers, and Charlotte the network. Craig spoke aloud to no one in particular, shouting out the discounts of the day: ten percent off on two-color banners, buy one get one free on sports pennants, new customer thirty-dollar discount on six feet or larger storefront signage. Buzz piled the early morning shipments next to the freight docks, and Harold was pouring himself his third cup of coffee when a young woman pushed through the front door.

"My sister," she said. "She's missing."

The woman looked frantic. She was young, maybe early twenties. She had been crying. Eyes purple and puffy. Cheeks stained. She wore a University of Central Oklahoma sweatshirt and couldn't catch her breath. At first, everyone in the store froze in shock. In the forty-two years that he'd run the place, Harold hadn't seen anything like it. The most excitement they'd ever had was when they'd found a squirrel in the warehouse tearing up inventory about a decade back. Other than that, days passed by in relative peace and quiet.

Susan got to her first. She held the young woman up, telling her oh honey, oh sweetheart, and patting her on the back while leading her to a chair. The whole store gathered around. Charlotte got the woman a cup of coffee, and after she calmed down a bit she told them her story.

Her name was Sprout, her sister River, and they were identical twins, sophomores at UCO, living a block over at the Apple Tree Apartment Complex. Last night River had gone out on a blind date through Tinder, and didn't come home.

"It's a dating app," she explained. "And the cops won't help me. Said she has to be missing for twenty-four hours."

"Maybe she just had a good time," Craig said. "Stayed over at the guy's place."

"She would've called," Sprout said. "She would've let me know."

"Did you call her?"

"Her phone's dead."

"Did you try contacting the guy through the app?"

"He's deleted his profile."

Silence followed. Craig scratched the back of his head. Susan put in a dip. Charlotte flipped through papers on the desk, and Harold, despite not wanting to, felt relief—what luck, he thought, at least for a moment, everything wouldn't be about him.


SPROUT HAD A PICTURE OF River. It was a recent one, taken at homecoming a couple of weeks back. She looked happy in it. Her smile wasn't forced or contrived, plastered on her face for the benefit of a picture. It truly was genuine. There was just no way to fake that kind of happiness. Harold tried to remember back when he'd last been that happy, and it took him a while to pinpoint a time. Probably the birth of his grandbaby, Eva, eight years ago. He'd been happy since, sure, when they had a good year at the store or when the Thunder had a deep run in the playoffs, but it wasn't face-aching happiness. He hadn't been bursting with joy to the point he couldn't help but smile. It was just there, small waves of pleasure, bookended by years and years of mundane contentment. And now he'd have to face retirement. Dear God, he thought. How would he spend his time? Playing backgammon?

Mack printed Sprout some flyers with River's name, height, weight, a description of what she'd been wearing and her last known whereabouts: Cheever's. It was a nice restaurant a few miles south. One of Harold's favorites, it had a chicken-fried steak to die for. Jalapeño gravy and breading, it could literally change a life. They figured that'd be the best place to start.

"You really don't have to help me," Sprout said. "Honest. I'll be fine by myself."

"Nonsense," Harold said. "Happy to help."

Harold feigned his motivations were altruistic, but they weren't. Really, he was just glad for an excuse to leave the store, if only for a few hours. He wanted to avoid the long eyes of Susan and Charlotte, mourning him as if he suffered from terminal cancer, and the pained expression of Mack, clacking his computer as if he wished to hurt the keys. Most of all, he desired nothing more than to avoid the gleeful prancing of Craig. Despite his best intentions, he couldn't help but resent his son-in-law. He knew he shouldn't, but Craig had put zero risk into the business, never having to spend long nights worrying whether he'd be able to sign enough customers to pay the bills, to keep the lights on, to feed his wife and daughter. He'd never know the sick, twisted feeling of failure, or the sweet taste of a pork chop after weeks of foregoing a good meal. Instead, with a flick of the pen, he'd have a nice little nest egg built in for him, a living and retirement married into. And Craig wouldn't let him forget, either.

"You'll be back to sign the papers, right?" he asked before Harold left with Sprout. "The attorney's supposed to be here by three."

"Wouldn't miss it for the world," Harold said.

Craig looked like he might swallow his tongue. "Okay. Just wanted to make sure. That's all."

It was cold out, but Harold didn't mind. He enjoyed it, actually. He'd spent his childhood in Iowa, in a little college town called Grinnell where his father had been a salesman for a local Anheuser-Busch distributor, and the winters there were frigid. Snow ten feet high at times. Ice hung from awnings. The entire landscape brilliant and sparkling. Nothing like the winters in Oklahoma. It hardly snowed that far south. Mostly, everything just died, turned brown and spindly, wind blowing so hard it gave him nosebleeds. It wasn't so bad that morning, though. It could even been called nice out.

"I can't tell you how much I appreciate this," Sprout said.

"Don't mention it," he said.

He got in his ten-year-old Honda Accord, and Harold fired up the engine. Sprout hesitated before sitting, though, standing there staring at the seat, at the floorboards, into the backseat.

"I won't hurt you," he said, immediately regretting it. He feared it sounded worse than saying nothing, but it seemed to work. Sprout got in the car, buckled her seat belt, and they headed for Cheever's.

It was a small place. Decades before, it had been a flower shop. The owners had lived in an attached residence in the back, and sold roses to lovers and tulips to the aggrieved. Harold remembered the store, had been a patron a few times even. Valentine's Day. An anniversary. His wife had always loved fresh flowers in the house, God rest her soul. This early in the morning, the restaurant wasn't open yet, so Harold had to knock on the front door. Not once, but three times.

A young kid opened the door.

"A manager in?" Harold asked.

The kid looked confused, perturbed even.

"Listen, kid. A girl's missing." Harold handed him a flyer. "Can we please speak with your manager?"

The kid took the flyer and let them in.

"Wait here," he said, and then disappeared into the back.

The front house lights were off, chairs upside down on the tables. Sprout walked around the dining area as if trying to glean some type of clue. The way she looked so earnestly, Harold half expected her to find something, a smoking-gun piece of evidence like in those police procedurals his late wife used to like to watch. Sprout reminded him of her in a way. It wasn't so much her appearance. Sprout was the typical blond-haired, blue-eyed American girl, a strange contrast to his wife's Lebanese olive skin and black hair. But her demeanor was familiar. She seemed mesmerized with the world, as if she could see things no one else could.

Harold's phone rang. It was his daughter, Sharon. He muted the ring and put his phone back into his pocket. It wasn't that he was ignoring his daughter; it was just he didn't want to talk with her right then. Lately, since he'd announced that he would, finally, retire, after all these years after his wife's passing, after so many years of Sharon asking him to, she'd started planning. She planned for vacations to the Boston Tea Party site and the new Ford Explorer she wanted to buy and the private school she wanted to put Eva into. It was like she'd already decided how she was going to spend his money after he died.

"How can I help you?" the manager asked. He was young, red-faced, unshaven. He stunk of booze and his eyes were bloodshot. He was clearly hungover.

Sprout told him the story.

"The guy's name is Chuck Marlon. I was thinking, maybe if he paid with a credit card—"

"We can't release any customer information without a court order."

"Or if someone remembered them? Saw what car they got into? What direction they went."

"I can ask around, but the waitstaff won't be in until later today. A lot who worked last night don't even work today."

"Call them in. An emergency meeting. Something."

"It's their day off, lady."

"My sister is missing! *Please.* Won't you help?"

"And I'm real sorry about that. I am, but I'm not the cops."

"Listen," Harold said. "This is serious here. A girl could be in danger."

"Like I said, buddy. I'm real sorry about that. I am. But what do you expect *me* to do about it?"

THEY LEFT A DOZEN OR so flyers with the manager to hand out to the staff and placed one at the hostess table for the guests to see, but it was all they could do. Once outside, Sprout tried her sister's phone again, but it went straight to voicemail. She left another message, her voice full of worry and angst, clinging to a vestige of hope. When she hung up, she tried social media, posting to her and her sister's Facebook page, asking anyone anywhere to let her know if they heard anything. As soon as she typed it, her phone lit up with messages of condolences and promises to keep their eyes open, the offerings of thoughts and prayers, but nothing tangible. No reported conversations. No sightings. Nothing.

"I don't know what to do," she said. "I feel so helpless."

"Let's put up flyers," he said. "Let's stay busy."

She nodded. They stayed together and walked up and down 36th Street. Used to, it had been the hippy hangout in the city, a place where Harold could score a little weed to share with his wife after a long day at the shop. Now it was full of tattoo parlors, chipped-paint dive bars, and dilapidated old theaters. A few developers had taken notice of the area in recent years and had started to inject some capital into it, so there were pockets of up-scale retail outlets and restaurants, but it was slow going. Many of the tenants were fighting the so-called gentrification of the neighborhood, their rents becoming unaffordable because of it. Harold didn't blame them for this. They'd been there for years and years and years, and now they were told to either pay up or move on. It wasn't a welcoming feeling, being told to leave after spending so much of your life there. Downright heartbreaking. But then again, it was good for the city, wasn't it? Progress?

They started out with the stores on the streets, asking businesses if they could put up the flyers on their doors. Most agreed. Even gave them the tape to stick them to the glass. Some said no, though. Young people mostly, clerks who feared their bosses' reprimands for making a decision on their own. Outside, most of the people they handed the flyers to were uninterested. They either walked on past without even looking at them, or they discarded them in the nearest trashcan they could find. Some feigned interest. Women mostly. Older. Ones who had lost someone before. Harold could tell in the way their faces would pucker up when they read the flyer, eyes and mouths and cheeks turning inward as if their bodies were trying to keep themselves together. "Oh, sweetie," they'd say. "Oh, honey. I am so, so sorry."

Turned out, Sprout's parents lived out of state. "That's why they aren't here," she said. "In case you were wondering." Harold was, he had to admit. Young kids like this, he figured the first call Sprout would've made would be to her parents. Then again, maybe not. He didn't know their relationship. Could be she feared their response, the backlash of anger and resentment rather than comfort and concern.

"They moved to the Virgin Islands right after we graduated from high school," she said.

"That must be nice."

She shrugged. "We've only been once. Dad opened up a company down there. The government is giving him a tax break to do it. Employ eight people, give some money to local charities, and they'll give you a ninety percent tax break."

"Not a bad deal."

"More like legal money laundering."

"So that's where they're at now?"

Sprout nodded, handed a flyer to man passing by. He grabbed it and looked at it, but he didn't stop. He didn't even slow. Just kept on marching down the street without breaking stride.

"You might want to give them a call. Let them know what's going on." Harold immediately regretted saying it. Wasn't his place to meddle in Sprout's family affairs. "Who knows, maybe they've heard from her?"

Harold's phone rang again, and again it was his daughter. He wasn't ready for that conversation just yet. He declined the call, and put his phone back into his pocket. It immediately buzzed again.

"You can get that," Sprout said.

"It's unimportant."

"Really, I don't mind."

"You don't think your sister would've called your parents?"

"Doubtful."

"You don't talk often?"

"We don't get in their business, and they don't get in ours."

"That's sad."

"It isn't anything."

"A family should be close."

"It is what it is."

"They're still your parents."

"Can we just stop talking about it? Please?"

Harold dropped it, and continued to hand out flyers to strangers who didn't care. The search was fruitless, but it was best to do something, Harold supposed, rather than nothing. Idleness bred hopelessness. He didn't know much, but he did know that.

For about an hour they continued, moving from 36th to 23rd to 10th. In midtown, the streets were cleaner, the shops newer, little apartment complexes housing young, affluent professionals walking dogs and drinking from tall, steaming coffee cups. He and Sprout were already low on flyers, and they were a few blocks away from the store when his phone rang for the fourth time. It was his daughter, again. He wasn't going to answer it, but Sprout stared at him expectantly. In a strange impulse not to disappoint her, he answered.

"Where are you?" Sharon asked.

"Craig didn't tell you?"

"He did. Some missing girl. But Dad, this day was supposed to be important."

Harold raised a finger to Sprout, indicating it would be a second, and took a few steps down the street.

"This is important, too, Sharon."

"You know what I mean," she said, her tone biting, accusatory even. "We were supposed to have a party. We were supposed to celebrate. God, Dad. Sometimes, I don't even know what to do with you anymore."

He loved his daughter. He did. But sometimes she could be dramatic. High strung. Selfish. Even as a child she'd been this way. Her mother refused to see it, but it was there, simmering just below the surface. Harold remembered a birthday party one year— she must've been about eight or nine—at a splash pad at a local park. Harold had forced her to invite every kid from her class, even though there were a couple she didn't care to include, a little girl by the name of Denise, especially. Denise was a quiet girl, nerdy, prone to walking pneumonia and clumsiness, and she didn't have many, if any, friends.

"It'll be social suicide," Sharon had said before the party. "Please, don't make me invite her."

But he did, and about an hour into the party, he regretted it. The girls, led by Sharon, had circled Denise in the middle of the splash pad so that the parents couldn't see her from the edge. It was there they held her down, pulled her chin back, and poured water down her nostrils, simulating drowning. Later, Harold would hear of this practice called waterboarding, torture even, but that day he called it the only thing he knew: frightening.

"I'll be back soon," he said. "A young woman needed help."

"That's what the police are for!"

Harold heard yelling behind him. A woman's voice. He couldn't quite make out the words—they were muddled, broken, syllables jumbled and incoherent.

"Please," Harold said. "Please don't do this, Sharon."

"Do what?"

"You know what."

"No, Dad. I don't. Do what? Expect you to spend time with your family? On the day of your retirement? For you to once do what you promised you would do? Why would I ever do a thing like that, Dad?"

The screaming became clearer, more coherent. It was Sprout screaming, and her tone was panicked. Something was wrong.

"I have to go, Sharon."

"Dad. Don't. Listen. Dad. Dad! Answer me!"

Sprout took off sprinting. People were staring now, jumping out of Sprout's way. She flailed her arms as she ran, screaming for somebody to stop, hey, stop that man, he had her sister. Harold followed, slowly at first, making his way through confused and startled passersby, but then he spotted him. He was blond, young, cheeks red, hair disheveled, clothes wrinkled. He looked sleep-deprived, hungover, and scared. He took off running, but Sprout had already hit her stride and soon came up on him, jumped on his back. He went down, and so did she, and as soon as they hit the ground, she started to punch and to kick and to bite.

"Where is my sister? Where is she? What did you do with her?!"

Harold reached them. The man was trying to say something, but Harold couldn't understand him over Sprout. She straddled him, and he lay on his side in the fetal position, forearms shielding his face from Sprout's clenched-fist blows. A crowd started to gather. No one was there to help. A few of them filmed the fight with their phones, laughing and egging Sprout on. Kick his ass, they yelled. Dude was getting beat up by a girl.

"What did you do with her, you sick fuck?!"

Harold pulled her off of him. She was strong and angry, and he had a hard time holding her back. The guy rose to his knees and then to his feet. His balance seemed off, and he held his head with his right hand.

"What the fuck is wrong with you?" the man asked.

Sprout went for him again, and this time Harold's grip slipped. She swung at the man, and he raised his arms to block the blow. Then it happened. The man pushed Sprout, hard enough to knock her to the ground. Her head cracked against the pavement, and she grimaced in obvious pain. Everyone looked shocked. The bystanders looked shocked. The man looked shocked, but it didn't matter. Harold punched him right in the face, connected on the apex of his cheekbone. Harold could feel the bone underneath. It was spongier than he had expected, more malleable, like it absorbed his fist by bending in on itself.

The man stumbled backward, and Harold pounced. He swung again, and again, and again, until the man fell to the ground. Harold jumped atop him, and his face was getting harder now, more calloused, wetter. Blood covered his face, his left eye closed, and again Harold swung, and again Harold swung, until his knuckles hurt and Sprout yelled at him to stop, stop, please, just stop.

Harold did. He stood, and he was breathing heavily. Dizzy. Disoriented. Couldn't tell if the blood on his hand was his own or the man's.

Sprout grabbed the man's shirt and pulled him to a sitting position, yelling, "Where is my sister? Where is she? Tell me where she is!"

"At my place! Okay? She's trying to get away from you! Is that what you want to hear? She's running away from *you*."

Sprout let him go, and he scooted backward and stood, cussing Sprout, cussing Harold, calling them crazy. Bat-shit nuts. No wonder River wanted to just disappear. He pushed through the crowd and continued down the street. Sprout remained sitting on the pavement. The man's blood covered her hands, her sweatshirt. After a little bit, the spectators lost their interest and dispersed as quickly as they'd arrived. Harold went to help Sprout to her feet, but she declined.

"Just leave me here," she said, and Harold did.

When Harold returned to Rainbow Pennant, everyone was there: Mack, Craig, Susan, Charlotte, Buzz, and Sharon. They looked shocked when he pushed through the door. He hadn't seen himself since the fight, but he imagined he looked strange. The blood for sure. It was everywhere. But that didn't bother him so much. His hands did, though. They hurt. They throbbed, actually, and he was afraid they might be broken. He could feel them swelling, and he couldn't quite make a fist with either of them anymore.

"Jesus, Dad. Oh my God. What happened?"

His daughter ran to him.

"It's nothing."

"Nothing? Look at you."

His employees didn't say a word. Craig looked at him like he was afraid. Mack seemed amused. Happy even. He smiled, and he raised a fist in the air like he was proud of Harold. He thought this strange, but he smiled back at Mack just the same.

"I'm tired," Harold said. "That's all."

"That's all? That's *all*? Today was an important day, Dad. A happy day. Everyone's here. And you've been gone all day. *All* day. And you come back looking like this? I baked a cake, for Christ's sake."

"The cake? That's what you're worried about?"

"That's not what I mean, and you know that."

"Not that I'm hurt. Or someone else could be hurt. Your first thought is the cake?"

"Dad, you're not hearing me right."

"Where's the cake, then? Where is it?"

Harold looked around. It wasn't in the showroom. It wasn't in the break room. He found it in his office atop his desk. White cake with white icing, it said, "Happy Retirement, Harold. Here's to the Golden Years." Next to it was the contract, bequeathing the store to his daughter, and to her husband.

"This is what you wanted? For us to eat cake?"

Harold grabbed a handful of cake and jammed it into his mouth.

"Dad, there's no reason for this."

He had to admit it was good. Vanilla, a subtle hint of cinnamon. Cream cheese icing. He grabbed another handful and jammed it into his mouth, chewing loudly, letting her see him enjoy it.

"Dad, please. Just stop."

"Anyone else want some?"

He held his hand out. Mack came in and grabbed a handful. Then Susan. Buzz. They all did. No fork. No plates. Just their hands and their mouths and icing all over their faces. Handful after handful, Craig and Sharon simply staring at them as if in disbelief. Harold picked up the contract. It was a short thing, ten, maybe fifteen pages at most, what his entire life's work boiled down to, an enumeration printed on legal-sized paper, wrought together by some pimply faced kid barely out of law school. He stopped when he found the signature block. There was his name printed in twelve-point Times New Roman, right above the words "President, Rainbow Pennant." He dipped his finger into the icing until he had a good amount dolloped at the end, then signed the contract with one quick swoop.

# *Life Expectancy*

THE JOB WAS IN OKLAHOMA, AND THE
WIND THERE WAS SOMETHING UNFORGIVEABLE. IT WAS HARD-
ened, stubborn, biting, and it blew across the plains so hard I
thought gravity an unequal match. I'd never experienced anything
like it. It drowned out all other noise. It roared. It whistled. It
taunted me, reminding me how small and inconsequential I truly
was. For a time, I was convinced I could bottle it up, that I could
take it with me, and if I faced something daunting, I could unleash
the wind upon it, and whatever it was would be destroyed. Silly, I
know, but that's how damn hard that wind blew.

I got the job through a friend of my brother's. I'd be working
for a young entrepreneur named Sayer, a bald-headed adrenaline
junkie who got rich through his buy-here, pay-here auto dealer-
ships and who was buying up life insurance contracts on the old
and dying.

"Ninety-eight percent of life insurance policies lapse," he told
me, standing on the outskirts of Duncan, Oklahoma, this blue-
collar town reeling from depressed oil and gas prices. The land
was dotted with abandoned wells, parked trucks, and crumpled

Busch cans, all shining underneath the midsummer sun. "That means these life insurance companies, these bloodsucking large conglomerates, take these hardworking people's monthly premiums year after year, then as soon as they can't pay, their policies are cancelled. Those poor bastards pay thousands of dollars over years and then poof, their investment is gone, surrendered to the pockets of strangers who ride in private jets and drink eighteen-year-old Scotch for breakfast. It's not right. And that's why we're here to help."

There was a doctor with us, an old guy by the name of Dickinson, and he carried with him a bag full of equipment to give our clients a physical on the spot; that way he could estimate just how long our client may have to live. A "life expectancy evaluation," he called it, and it was essential to determine Mr. Sayer's return on investment. If the insured lived too long, Mr. Sayer might lose money. The three- to five-year window was the sweet spot. Pay the insured a percentage of the face value, have him or her sign over the beneficiary rights to Mr. Sayer, and he would continue to pay the premiums until the insured passed, hopefully sooner rather than later. Then Mr. Sayer would reap the rewards. He called them uncorrelated assets, investments that didn't rise or fall with the stock market. It was smart, I had to admit, yielding returns damn near triple digits if underwritten correctly.

The first call I ever went on was at a small house sitting on an acre. Ranches surrounded the lot, the lazy moos of cattle audible between wind bursts, the smell of cow pies stinging my nostrils. A drought had scourged the southwest part of the state in recent years, so the land was cracked, blades of grass burnt brown and crunching beneath my footsteps. Though it was a small house, it was well cared for and neat. I could tell it had started out much smaller. The owners had added on a couple rooms—one on the north side, another on the west—and there was a large, newly built detached garage. Out front was a modest pontoon, an F-250 Super Diesel, and a used, but still impressive, RV.

Mr. Hannahan greeted us at the door. Rotund but tall, he had a shiny hairless head and a granite mouth. He seemed gigantic, his head nearly touching the door frame. Inside, the house was dim, illuminated by uncovered bulbs, their light oscillating through lazy, undulating fans. Walls covered in floral wallpaper, stained with cigarette smoke. Ceilings low, popcorn textured. In the kitchen, Mrs. Hannahan stood nearly as tall as her husband, readying a tray of finger sandwiches.

"Forced retirement," Mr. Hannahan explained once we were all settled in the formal dining room, sipping on sugary iced tea. "Oil companies started laying off. Tax revenue went south. Thirty-seven years at the high school, and they told me during finals week this year would be my last. Should've saw it coming but didn't."

"We understand," Mr. Sayer said.

I was here to observe, that was all. Learn from Mr. Sayer, note his inflection, his concern, his empathy, so that I'd be able to do the same.

"Times are tough. You have to look out for your family. For your wife."

Mrs. Hannahan offered him a refill, and Mr. Sayer accepted

with a warm and friendly smile.

Dr. Dickinson began his physical, measuring blood pressure, heart rate, blood sugar, checking his pupils and listening to his lungs, testing them relative to the medical history we'd already studied. Mr. Hannahan had had his first heart attack seven years prior, his second just a year before our visit. High blood pressure, type 2 diabetes, still smoked a pack a day. We gave him two to three years tops, and he was sitting on a term life policy worth half a million with premiums inching up toward three grand a year. We offered him twenty grand to take that burden off his name.

"Upside down on the house. Upside down on the truck. Upside down on the RV. Can't hardly make the payments on my pension. It was stupid." He shook his head and stared at his drink like he was talking to it. "Stupid."

"You don't have a crystal ball. You aren't psychic. How were you supposed to see this coming?"

"Just stupid."

"But that's all about to change."

Mr. Sayer pushed over the contract. It was a short document, just ten pages long. A tab marked where Mr. Hannahan was to sign. He flipped through it, glancing over the terms and conditions, the fine print, masquerading as if he were reading it but not taking the time to fully understand. He then grabbed his pen and held it over the signature block, pausing for a moment like he was remembering how to sign his name, and put pen to paper in a short, quick stroke.

BEFORE THIS GIG, I'D HELD several jobs, never one that actually took: used car salesman, personal banker, fast-food restaurant GM. Each had its perks; each had its downfalls. Probably the worst was being a recruiter for Hertz. My job was to pack in as many bodies as possible, all on thirty- or sixty-day temp contracts. Their job was simple: to detail the cars. I'd find these kids all over by trolling Facebook for anyone complaining they were out of work. Bail bondsmen would send me referrals, kids who'd been arrested for public intox or street racing. All of them were desperate; all of them needed something to hold on to. And so that's what I sold them, stability. A chance for them to better themselves.

Problem was it hardly ever turned out that way. The company I worked for, Singular Temp Associates, had a cash flow problem. A year prior, their CEO had been sued over a commercial real estate deal that went south, and he had a judgment placed against him. That left him with his revolving line of credit called due but a contract to fulfill. He had temps to pay in thirty days, but Hertz didn't pay until sixty, a problem he never was able to fix.

The kid who got to me the worst was a boy named Eddie. Seventeen years old, he'd been busted for a B&E a couple of months prior. Wasn't the kid's fault, really, if you believed his lawyer, just started hanging out with the wrong crowd, got dragged into something that wasn't his idea. We worked with the DA to get his charge reduced to a simple trespassing if he kept his job for ninety days and completed a year's probation. Day sixty-eight rolled around, Eddie didn't get paid, and so he quit. Couldn't blame the kid, working for nothing. This sprang the terms of his plea deal, though, and the kid wound up getting charged as an adult and spending a year behind bars. Once released, he showed up at my doorstep.

Eddie was a wiry kid, malnourished, the veins protruding from his arms an indigo blue. Wrapped in his hand was a crowbar.

"You fucked me," he said.

"I'm sorry."

"You stole a year of my life."

"I'm sorry. I really am."

Didn't matter though. Ended up with a four-inch laceration on my forehead, a black eye, a fractured cheekbone. I could've turned the kid in to the cops, got him sent back to the pen on an assault and battery charge, but I didn't. Instead I just made myself a promise: I'd never fuck anyone over like I had Eddie. Not knowingly, anyway.

My girlfriend at the time, Callie, collected vintage action figures and comic books, selling them to nerds throughout Oklahoma City and Tulsa, usually at trade shows or on Facebook. Pimply faced teenagers, middle-aged men reliving their childhoods, divorced dads looking for something cool to get their kids for their birthdays. It was a lucrative business, actually, hocking mint condition, still-in-the-box C3POs and Green Lanterns. She had nice things, smelled nice, drove a nice car, had a nice IRA. She was just a nice girl.

"You're not going to believe what happened to me today," she said. We were at dinner, celebrating my recent hiring, at this up-scale comfort-food joint called Cheever's. They had this jalape-ño chicken-fried steak that could change a life, but Callie never would order it, regardless of how many times we came, regardless of how many times I asked her to just try it.

"What do you think you're going to get?"

"I got a call from this guy, and he was looking to sell a Spawn #1. Mint condition. Never been out of its sleeve he said, and so I said sure, bring it down."

"Everything just looks so good." I flipped the page of the menu: smoked chicken fusilli, molasses roast chicken breast, five-spice trout.

"So I wait for this guy all day. Like all day. Finally, I get tired of waiting and decide to close up shop, but as soon as I go to lock the door, there he is."

"You've tried the chicken-fried steak, right?" I asked, even though I knew she hadn't.

"I tell him to come back tomorrow, but he gets all pissed off, screaming that it's like an hour drive for him to get here and blah blah blah, so I'm like fine, whatever, and let him in."

"It's so good. It's got jalapeño in the breading and gravy. You think it's going to be too spicy and heavy, but it really isn't. You should try it."

"So he shows me the comic, and it checks out. Spawn #1, great condition. Doesn't look like it's seen the light of day since the nineties, and even better, it's the newsstand edition, has the barcode on the front and everything, so I ask him how much he wants for it. Know what he says?"

"I really think you'd like it if you just gave it a chance."

"Twenty bucks! Can you believe that? I laughed at him, thinking he was joking at first, but he wasn't. This guy had no idea what he had. There's only like, maybe ten thousand of these puppies around, and he's just like *twenty bucks.*"

She made a voice like what she thought a stupid man sounded like, deep and guttural, cinching the last syllable up as if asking a question.

"So what'd you do?" I asked.

"I pulled up Amazon and showed him the comic store edition. Told him these only sold retail for ten or fifteen, that I could only offer him five."

"You did that? Really?"

"He was pissed at first. Started cussing right there in the store. Cussing somebody named Brett, cussing the comic book, even cussing me."

"But he took it, didn't he?"

She nodded. "And I'm going to turn around and sell it for $300."

She smiled, proud of herself, and I returned to the menu. She chewed some unbuttered bread, taking her time before swallowing. It was crowded in the restaurant, with little room between white-clothed tables. The lighting dim. Conversations hushed.

"So how do you like it so far?" she asked. "Your job. Is it good?"

"Sure," I said. "It's good."

"Oh? Just good?"

"Yeah."

"What's good about it?"

"I don't know."

"Just *good*?"

"It's a job."

"Do you like your boss? Do you like your clients? The travel? What exactly?"

"So what are you going to order?"

"Or maybe you just like the pay? It's okay to like a job just because it pays well."

"I haven't been paid yet."

"But you will," she said. "You will. It's just a matter of time before you make a sale."

She reached across the table to grab my hand, but it was too far to reach. She pulled her hand back and laid it in her lap.

"You really should try the chicken-fried steak," I said. "I know you'll like it. It's famous. Like really famous. Outside of Oklahoma even."

"I've been thinking," she continued. "You know, it doesn't make much sense for us to keep two places. Financially speaking. You're always either at my place, or I'm at yours. It just makes sense, right?"

"What does?"

"Moving in together."

"Like, *us*? Me and *you*?"

She cocked her chin to the side, mouth poised to respond, but before she could answer, the waiter came. He was a young kid, maybe early twenties, with a mustache trying too hard to make him look older. "Have any questions about the menu?"

"No," Callie said. "I think we're ready."

"And what'll it be?"

"The salmon," she said, snapping her menu shut.


FIRST TIME I WENT OUT by myself, the temperature reached almost 110 degrees. Luckily, I didn't have to wear a jacket or tie. I donned a simple cotton polo, some chinos, loafers without socks. Mr. Sayer encouraged us to stay pretty casual, said that clients tended to trust us more than if we constrained ourselves in suits.

I'd always had a problem with perspiration, though. No matter the clothing, I sweated. I soaked through my polo, my underwear, my pants, everything, until visible rings stained in inadvisable places. And I stunk. Regardless of how much cologne I wore, how much deodorant I applied, how hard I blew the air conditioner, I emanated a debilitating and nauseating body odor. I'd seen doctors and dermatologists and dieticians, trying to mask or cure it, applying topical solutions and eating more pineapple, but nothing worked. Finally, I just came to expect it, and the unrelenting scowls of strangers.

My first prospect was a rancher down in Empire, Mr. Cartwright. His place was sprawling, about three hundred acres of pasture, a couple barns, an ancient home passed down from generation to generation, from father to son since the Homestead Act.

When I arrived, the whole family was there. Father, son,

daughter, wife, aunts, uncles, grandparents, grandkids, cousins, nieces, nephews. They crawled over one another. They fed each other ham sandwiches and iced tea and hit each other over the head with hand-me-down toys. There must've been two dozen of the clan, all waiting, like this was some sort of family reunion rather than an estate-planning pitch.

They bid me sit at the dining room table. The adults all joined me there, the kids remaining in the family room making a racket. Once inside, I'd hoped my sweating would come under control, cooled by the air-conditioning, but with so many bodies jam-packed into such a tight space, I couldn't stop. It poured from me. It stung my eyes and made my vision blurry. It was so bad Mrs. Cartwright even offered to get me a fan.

"No thank you," I said. "I don't want to be any trouble."

"No trouble," she said. "Really. And there's no reason to be nervous. We won't bite." She winked.

"I'm sorry for the stench," I said.

"Can't smell a thing," she lied.

"Maybe I should just freshen up a bit."

"That might be wise."

Their bathroom was small, covered in sky-blue tile and pink towels. Elephant figurines dotted the windowsill, the sink rim, even the back of the toilet. The magazine rack housed decades-old *Sports Illustrated* and *National Geographic*, and everything was in its place: toothbrushes and hand soap and towels with the family name stitched into the fabric. It reminded me of my grandmother's home, before she'd lost her memory to Alzheimer's and we had to stick her in an assisted-living center outside Pawhuska, and I splashed my face with cool water and kept telling myself *I can do this, I can do this, I can do this.*

Back in the kitchen, I was greeted with handshakes and smiles and introductions, a glass of iced tea and questions. All types of questions.

"You're going to pay me $125,000 for my policy? Cash? Today?"

"Well, it'll be put in an escrow account. The funds will be wired to you after closing."

"Doesn't matter its cash value is only $100,000?"

"Nope."

"And you'll take over all the premiums? I won't have to pay a dime?"

"Not one cent."

"So what's the catch?"

The catch. That was a good one. I knew what Sayer would want me to say: there wasn't one. They had a policy they couldn't afford or didn't need, and we'd pay them for it. Problem was, that wasn't always the case. There were tax consequences, estate-planning implications, debt that would no longer be able to be retired after death. There was a whole host of concerns and questions they weren't grasping, or didn't even know to ask. The most glaring of all: we were going to profit off of their deaths. When they died, their family would get nothing. A stranger would, a bald-headed guy they'd never meet and who only thought of them as a line item on his balance sheet. They were relying upon me to tell them those things, but it was my job not to, and soon my shirt was soaked again in perspiration.

"Don't worry." Mrs. Cartwright patted me on the hand. "You're doing just fine."

PART OF MY JOB WAS calling the insured to see if they were still alive. I'd leave a message, and usually they'd call me back. Still kicking, they'd say, for a minute still. Sometimes, though, I wouldn't hear from them. I'd call two or three times over about a month's span, and if they didn't return my call, I'd have to go make a house visit.

After a while, we hadn't heard from Mr. or Mrs. Hannahan. It was a hot day, the sun burning the cracked, red clay of Oklahoma. Thermometer only said 98 but the heat index topped 110. Despite the air-conditioning blaring in my Honda Accord, every single part of me was covered in sweat. My arms, my neck, the insides of my thighs. It was so bad I stuck to my car interior. I thought I would, at any time, start melting.

Duncan looked exactly as it had several months prior. A sleepy town, it had more than once boomed and busted, but this past bust seemed to last longer than all the rest. Houses went unpainted, fences un-mended. The townsfolk took to just sitting. Sitting at the IGA, sitting at the high school football field, sitting on their front porches, all of them looking off into the distance.

I knocked on the Hannahans' front door. They had one of those old-timey brass knockers, and it felt strange using it, like

I might have unknowingly slipped into a former time. There was no answer. I knocked again, this time using my fist. I checked the windows, but the blinds had been drawn shut. I tried the back door. I tried calling. Still, no answer. I rang the doorbell, but no one came to the door. There wasn't even anything stirring on the other side.

Walking back to the street where I'd parked, I realized that the truck and the RV were gone but the boat remained. I stopped at the mailbox. It was full, stocked with furniture catalogues and credit card applications, mostly unpaid bills: their mortgage, their second mortgage, the RV, the pontoon, all stamped red, stating Third and Final Notice, Foreclosure Proceedings. It looked like no one had taken a thing for a couple weeks, and so I called the police.

"Come quick," I told them. "I think we may have a problem."

We found Mr. Hannahan sitting in his recliner. There was no sign of Mrs. Hannahan. He had a microwavable dinner on his lap, molding. The TV was still on, tuned to the local NBC affiliate, the volume turned low, barely audible. I found this odd. If I could barely hear it, then Mr. Hannahan likely would not have been able. It appeared he hadn't cared to hear the actors' voices—it had been enough just to see them, living their muted lives, filling in the details as he saw fit.

I MOVED INTO MY GIRLFRIEND'S apartment on a Saturday morning. It was unseasonably cool. A thunderstorm had moved through during the twilight hours of the morning, and the ground smelled wet and was unstable. The air felt like it vibrated, gravid with static electricity.

There was a guy walking down the street, picking through trash cans. Every time I unloaded a box and came outside to grab another, he'd be there, elbow deep. What he was looking for, I hadn't a clue. He didn't look homeless. He wore a newish-looking sweatshirt, not marred with stains or dirt. His jeans fit and were devoid of fray. His boots were a bit muddy, older, but not falling apart. Clean shaven. Recent haircut. But he just kept going through all the trashcans, never taking anything out, always picking up after himself if he accidentally spilled an item. It was the strangest thing I'd seen in a while, and I couldn't help but stop what I was doing and watch him.

"Do you think we should call the cops?" Callie asked.

"What?"

She pointed at the man. "The cops. He's freaking me out a little."

Maybe. But it didn't seem necessary. He might just be looking for something he'd lost, or had been stolen from him, or perhaps, in a momentary lapse of judgment, thrown out, and now he desperately searched every trash can on the street because he couldn't quite remember where he'd put it. That had to be it, I thought. He'd had a change of heart, and now he had to do whatever he could to get it back.

## Acknowledgements

Thank you first and foremost to my wife, Allie. This book wouldn't have been possible without you. A special thank you to the numerous editors at the literary magazines that previously published the stories in this collection, most notably Adam Van Winkle at *Cowboy Jamboree*, Kelly McMasters at *Windmill: The Hofstra Journal of Literature and Art,* and Hila Ratzabi at *Storyscape Literary Journal.* Lastly, thank you to my editor and publisher, Michelle Halket, for believing in my work.

Noah Milligan began his community banking career in 2008 in the midst of the subprime mortgage crisis. The resulting Great Recession shaped his professional and personal life as he witnessed firsthand the devastating toll it took on people from all rungs of the socioeconomic ladder as they lost their homes, their retirement, and their savings. His debut novel, *An Elegant Theory*, was shortlisted for the Horatio Nelson Fiction Prize and a finalist for Foreword Reviews 2016 Book of the year. His short fiction has appeared in *Windmill: The Hofstra University Journal of Literature and Art*, MAKE Literary Magazine, *Cowboy Jamboree*, *Rathalla Review*, and elsewhere.

noahmilligan.com

Printed in the United States
by Baker & Taylor Publisher Services